SOUVENIRS FROM ANOTHER LIFE

SOUVENIRS FROM ANOTHER LIFE

STORIES

LEAH BROWNING

Quiet Ocean Studio & Press

Published in the United States of America by Quiet Ocean Studio & Press, San José, California.

Names: Browning, Leah, author.
Title: Souvenirs from another life: stories / Leah Browning.
Trade paperback ISBN: 979-8-9990752-0-8
E-book ISBN: 979-8-9990752-1-5
Library of Congress Control Number: 2025911108
Short stories, American. | Short stories (single author). | Domestic fiction.

Front cover photograph by Jonathan Kemper.
Back cover photograph by Sarah Trummer.

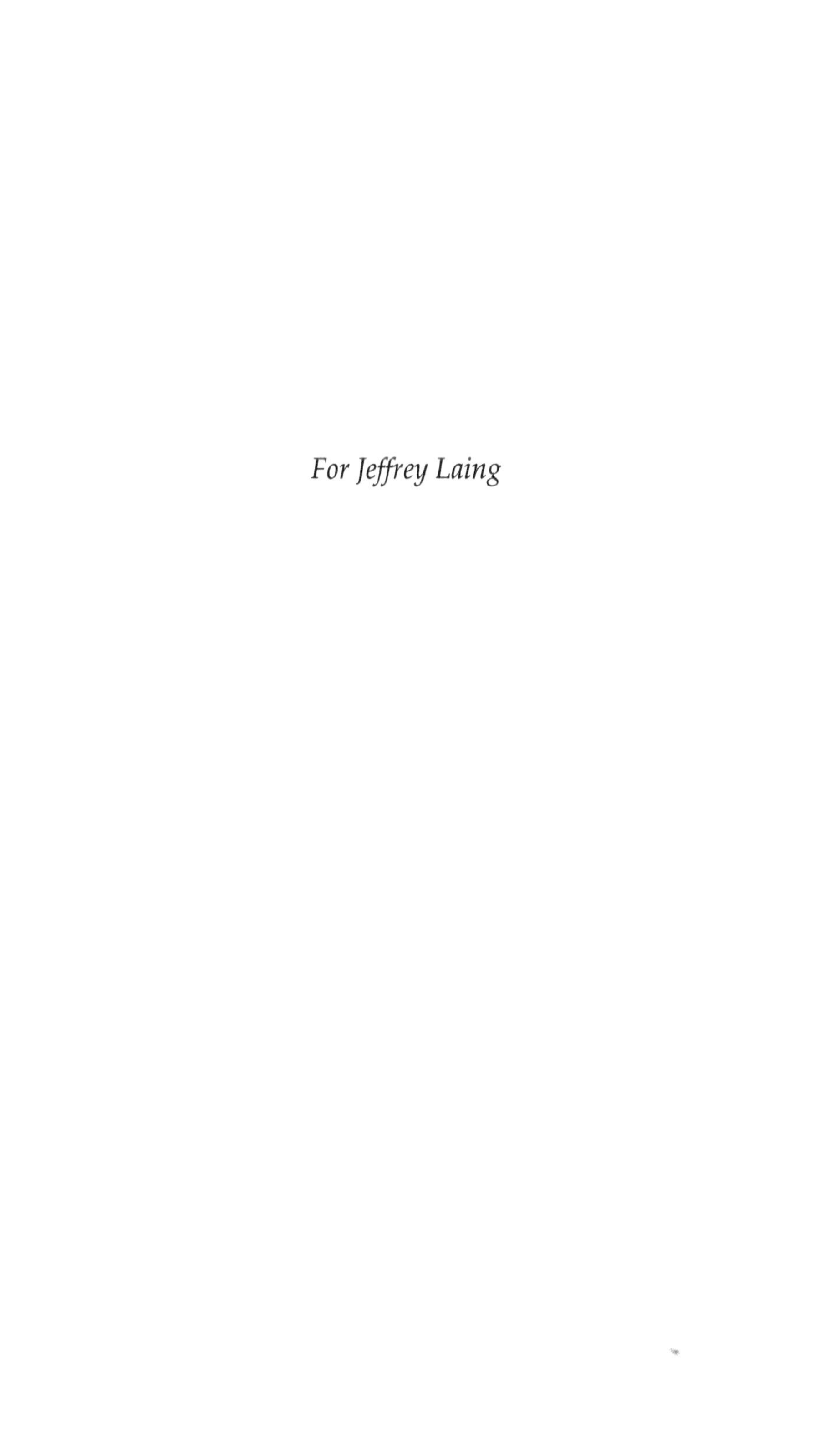

For Jeffrey Laing

Contents

SOUVENIRS FROM ANOTHER LIFE

PUNCH

First, there's an ultrasound. Or, no, that's not the beginning. First, there's a forgettable night with your husband. You've been married eight years already and the spark is gone—it's more than gone—its absence is so huge that it's become a presence in and of itself.

But you're not thinking about that anymore. You want a baby now. You're like the Marisa Tomei character in *My Cousin Vinny* where she's standing on the porch in a black bodysuit saying, "My biological clock is ticking like this," and pounding the wooden boards with her foot. The main difference is that you're not going to win an Academy Award for all the nights you've sat up in bed trying to wheedle your husband into agreeing that you should go off the pill.

It's not that he doesn't like children. When he holds your nephews on his lap or reads one of your nieces a storybook, he's so sweet it makes tears come to your eyes. It makes him emotional, too, but that's because he's still working at the copy shop and the novel he's been working on for ten years is unfinished and every short story he sends out comes back with a little scrap of paper with a preprinted rejection paperclipped to the front of the manuscript, and even though he loves books and he loves to read, it's gotten to the point that by the time he leaves a bookstore, he's so depressed he seems like he wants to die.

And it doesn't help that you were laid off last year, which seemed like perfect timing baby-wise because you're thirty-eight now and you're not getting any younger and every magazine article you read seems to trumpet this fact and a bunch of others that you'd rather not think about, but now money is tighter than ever and even though he's a year younger than you are, he's still cruising toward forty and his twenty-year high school reunion is next year and he's more of a failure than ever. It's a sad speech, but you've heard it ten trillion times because you've been friends since college, back when he was still sure that things would work out. He's not even bitter anymore—just resigned.

So you borrow a little money from your mom. You help him get a new suit and a new job that has longer hours but has better pay and benefits. You take your temperature and make a chart to see when you're ovulating and eat well and take folic acid. You haven't taken a drink in six months. After a few tries, you're so bored by the idea of sex with your husband that you want to cry. The movies and the sitcoms that make sex-for-the-sole-purpose-of-a-baby look like a chore are dead-on.

The problem is that you don't get pregnant, and you don't get pregnant, and then the teenage girl in the little house two doors down from yours does get pregnant and her mother starts wearing a baseball cap low over her eyes and pretending she doesn't see anyone she knows at the grocery store. You call your doctor friend and you do cry while she explains why the high school sex ed. classes make it seem like you can practically get pregnant by brushing up against someone of the opposite sex, but when you're older and settled and actually want a baby, it just doesn't seem to happen.

You don't have a job to go to anymore so you lie on the couch sometimes and look out the window and think about your body like an old refrigerator and your eggs which are just inside rotting. You seem to spend a lot of time crying. But then you pull yourself up by your bootstraps (as your father would have said) and go for long walks and volunteer to watch your friend's son because his nursery school has a weeklong break while she and her husband have to work.

The little boy likes to drive his Matchbox cars around on the carpet or color or play with a big, elaborate dollhouse passed down from his older sister. After the first few days, he does these things alone while you lie on the couch, resting. You want to be happy but you've started to throw up every hour on the hour, or something like that. You've got morning sickness, afternoon sickness, and evening sickness. Sometimes, if you lie very still and don't eat anything but saltines, you might get a two-hour break. At first, as you kneel in front of the toilet, the little boy is standing next to you, patting you on the back and crying a little, but by the last day of the nursery school break he only looks up and gives you a sympathetic nod as you head back to the bathroom.

Finally you get to the ultrasound. It feels like a new beginning because you're finally starting to show, and you've finally stopped having the taste of vomit in your mouth no matter how many times you brush your teeth. It's the most contented you've ever felt even though you have incessant heartburn and a jag of pain radiating down one leg. When the technician points to the black and white images on the screen and says, "It looks like you're having a boy," and your husband squeezes your hand and smiles, you think that you would live with sciatica for the rest of your life if it meant you would have a happy family.

And for a while, you do.

The baby's born. Your husband gets very emotional and cuts the umbilical cord with a pair of giant silver scissors and takes a bunch of pictures of you holding the baby in your arms even though all you can see is the hospital blanket with an anonymous baby's nose poking out of it and your giant face with all its blood vessels burst from the hours of pushing. You're all torn up and stitched up and drugged up, and then when you get home, the baby spends all night crying and you think, *Oh my god what have I gotten myself into—I am way too old for this.*

Your breasts are sagging, your stomach is sagging, and your hair is falling out in your hands when you manage to take a shower and when you look down at the strands, most of them are gray. You're afraid suddenly that people will think the baby is your grandson.

Every once in a while, when you were younger, you used to wonder why mothers let themselves go, but now you understand. You don't have time to brush your hair, and you wear your glasses because your eyes ache at the mere thought of having contacts jammed into them, and you wear sweatpants to the grocery store because you just don't care anymore. In fact, you run into the teenage mother from down the street buying formula and tiny glass jars of food for her baby (who looks like a giant compared to your baby!) and she's also wearing gray sweatpants, but she's lost all the baby weight and looks cute and perky with her hair up in a little ponytail and the word SWEET sewn across the seat of her pants.

But still, there are these moments when you're happier than you've ever been, when the baby falls asleep and drools onto your wrist and you feel so much love for him you think you just can't take any more. Your husband is just as bewitched, and he takes hundreds of photos of the baby napping or staring into space, and he sends fat files of them to everyone you both know.

You give the baby a good childhood. You color and play with Matchbox cars and dolls. You take the kid to play group and library storytime and friends' houses. Some of his friends are third or fourth children, and the parents have kind of pooped out, but you're getting enough sleep again and you've always been a determined person, so when he shows some interest, you sign him up for soccer and T-ball and teach him a little Spanish.

In exchange, you're so richly, embarrassingly rewarded. You have drawers filled with cut paper hearts, "I ♥ MOM" painstakingly printed in crayon, and all his drawings and letters and intense unabashed love. When you lean over his bed at night to kiss his candy-smelling head and he smiles and reaches up his little arms to squeeze your neck, you know that the privilege of being his mother is worth every second of worry and stress and mind-numbing boredom.

After his last year of elementary school, you think you might try to dip your toe back into the job market, but you haven't kept up with computer technology and now you need new training. You had thought that you'd go back when he was much younger, but there was always so much to do, and you'd barely have dropped him off at school when it was time to go pick him back up. Your husband is still looping a tie around his neck every morning and going to a job that he hates but that has good benefits. You remind him of this when he's moping, which is pretty much all the time, and honestly, you would leave him if you thought things would be better somewhere else but the boy needs his father and anyway you're fifty now and where exactly do you think you're going to go on your little varicose veined legs?

So first, there's a night with your husband, and in the end, there's a bathroom door. It's not really the end, or even the beginning of the end, but it does seem like it at the time. Your son has grown into a teenager and he's suddenly shy, or maybe withdrawn; you're not sure which. Girls start to call the house, and there's a shadow of dark hair on his upper lip, and one evening you are walking up the stairs with a basket of clean laundry and you catch him coming out of the bathroom, freshly showered, with only a towel wrapped around his waist, and he edges past you impatiently, irritably. He can't wait to get away from you.

You tell him to do things—unload the dishwasher, go to his room—and for the first time since he was a toddler, he raises his chin and says no, and when he takes a step toward you, you're aware of him suddenly in a way you never were before; he's almost the same height, there are visible muscles in his arms, and there is a sickening, unsettling feeling in your stomach, an understanding that physically, you're now pretty evenly matched. You remember learning in school all those years ago about the concept of a paradigm shift.

Night after night, stress dreams. It's raining outside, the roof is leaking, the pots you place under the leaks fill with water, everything is overflowing. Or the man down the street who has always given you the creeps is standing on his front porch, barefoot, in a pair of suit pants and a short-sleeved white undershirt staring at you as you walk by, which he often does in real life, and now when you rush past his house, the sinister undertone has become an overtone, and even though he has always seemed creepy but harmless you find yourself wondering if there is something more to the story.

But that's just a way to take your mind off your own home, which you've arranged so carefully but which seems to be unraveling. There are so many things to argue about: wet towels on the bathroom floor, or on the hardwood of your son's bedroom, or hung over a burning lamp; music played too loudly; a report card where the high point is a single C. You and your husband spend hours bickering over what to do about this problem, that problem. Your son slouches around with his hair in his eyes as if he wants to blend into the walls. Just hearing him come home after school sets your teeth on edge. You'll be in the kitchen preparing dinner or in your home office paying the bills, and you'll hear the front door and then the door of his bedroom slamming one after the other.

You've been having trouble making yourself get out of bed in the morning, and sometimes it takes a lot of effort to push back the desk chair and stand up. You try not to think about anything in particular. You and your husband have taken away his skateboard and headphones, unplugged the computer, and banned the television, and it is unfair. He hates you. He will always hate you and he can't wait until he's eighteen and he can get out of this house. That's not quite what he says word for word, but that's the gist of it.

So when you knock on the door, twice, and he finally barks, "What?" your impulse is to turn away, but you steel yourself and say in your best kindergarten teacher voice that you hope he had a good day at school and could he please come out and unload the dishwasher and sweep the kitchen before he gets started on his homework. Please.

You try to sound pleasant yet commanding, but he seems to find you unpleasant and un-commanding—feeble, you might even say—and he practically knocks you down as he opens the door and sweeps past you. He's going to a friend's house and he's not doing any of these stupid chores before he leaves, either. He can't wait until he's eighteen and he can leave this house and never come back.

This is starting to sound good to you, too. But you stand up straighter and say, "You're not going anywhere," and he glares at you, absolutely radiating anger, and says, "I'd just like to punch you in the face," but then jerks away from you, swearing, and puts his hand through a wall.

Somehow you end up in the bathroom, sitting on the edge of the tub with the door locked and your head in your hands. You can no longer hear him in the rest of the house and you don't know where he is. You know now that he is going to be a thief or a drug dealer or a serial killer, or maybe all of the above, and he's going to systematically ruin your life if he doesn't hack you to death with a meat cleaver or shoot you in your sleep, and you think about getting locks for the bedroom doors or sending him away or murdering him for his own good before he can murder you first. You've never been one of those women who thinks that men are scum; you've known a lot of good, steady men in your life, including his father, who is probably at this very moment sitting at a desk filing paperwork so that this boy can continue to have a roof over his head and food on the table; and thinking of your husband giving up his dreams, thinking of everything you both have given up, makes you weep. But the boy doesn't know anything. These aren't his memories.

There is a faint knock. He's saying, "Mom?" and in his voice you can hear it all—the remorse, the apology, the need for forgiveness. That's not all, though; there's so much more left, and you don't want to do this anymore, you don't know if you have the energy to keep on going—it's too much, it's just too much!—but he continues knocking, and eventually

you wipe your eyes and stand up and walk across the bathroom and open the door again.

SKIN

I told Jeremiah I knew of a place where we could go.

It's out a ways in the woods, I said. A cabin where the people that own it don't hardly spend any time. They have more than one house and don't need this one so much.

It took us almost half an hour to walk up there. I'd heard there was only a few houses around, and this one was all by its lonesome. We tried to be quick, looking like we knew where we were going.

The doors were locked, but one of the windows had a broken latch. Jer just pushed it in, didn't need to break the glass or nothing.

It was dark inside. Outside, there was still some light, but you couldn't tell it once you got in the house. I was afraid to turn on any lamps. The house was pretty far back from the road, but you just never know who might be watching.

After a second, my eyes got used to the dark. I could see all these creepy pictures on the walls, the kind where it's of a person, and the eyes of that person follow you around the room. I tried not to look at them. The whole thing was giving me a bad feeling, if you want to know the truth. I was afraid Jer would try to spook me, put a cold hand on the back of my neck or something like that, but I could tell he didn't like those following eyes any better than I did.

We went upstairs. The place was starting to feel like a witch house to me, but upstairs was different, not so dark, with a lot of them windows in the roof and a lot of plants all over the place. I couldn't understand why they didn't die without water, but when Jeremiah went to look around downstairs, I touched one, and then I knew that it stayed alive because it was fake, not cheap plastic but silk or something like that. I put my fingers on the leaves, feeling them.

Between the windows, the walls were all wood, all around the room, and there was a table off to the side with a bowl full of wood fruit. Wood apples painted a dark red. You had to look close to see that nothing in the room was real.

Behind the couches and tables there were more plants painted onto the back walls, and painted-on bookshelves full of painted-on books. In front of the couches, in the middle of the floor, was a big white bearskin rug.

I stopped eating meat a long time ago, and I hated the idea of a bear like that. I didn't think it was real, though, if you want to know the truth. I could touch the spines of the books on the wall and they were just stripes of colored paint on the wood. The books were big ones, things you would have heard of, like Shakespeare and them, but then you couldn't open them or nothing, so what was the point, if you know what I mean.

But the bear turned out to be a real bear after all. I put my hand on that white fur and it was so soft, and there was a head and everything, with eyes and a face. It killed me to see that. It had a real soft-looking face, too, like it wouldn't hurt a fly, even though before it was dead it was probably real fierce or something, not so soft as all that.

I couldn't stop touching it, and when Jeremiah came back he said what was I doing, on my knees next to the edge of the fur, petting it like it was a dog or something. He put his hand on it, too, though, and felt how it was. All soft-like. I couldn't find anything good, he said. They must not keep nothing here when they leave. Not even any clothes in the closets. Nothing in the drawers.

I wasn't surprised. These people's rich, but they're not going to go back to their regular everyday house and leave no diamond necklace in a cabin. It just don't make sense. Jeremiah doesn't use his head, sometimes, though, so he thought they might. He opened all the drawers in all the bedrooms, still thinking there was a chance, never mind that all the ones he'd already done were empty.

You should take off your clothes, he said, and I said, What? Still thinking about rich people's jewelry.

This fur is so soft, he said. It makes me want to lay on it with you. He was on his haunches, but then he sat down on the bear's skin and patted his hand on its back. Sit down, he said.

I shook my head.

It was one thing to lie on the floor, or even sleep in the house, which was what my plan was from the get-go, but I wanted to let that bear alone.

He just wouldn't stop, though, grabbing me round the waist and pulling me down on top of him. Where's the stuff, I said, and he said, Don't worry, baby. It's right here. I got everything you need.

I didn't like it when he talked like that. That's the kind of talk my mama hates out of him, or any man, but I tried not to think about her just then. I pulled away from him. He sighed, but he got everything ready. I held real still. It took him two tries to get the vein, and it hurt like the devil, but then it was okay.

After, we lay on the rug and I let him take off my jeans. The fur was so soft you couldn't believe it. I lay there in my bra and underwear. It was almost pitch black by that time and the shape of my underwear looked real dark against that white bear fur.

Jeremiah was pressing himself all up against me, rubbing his legs on mine, and I could feel my pulse, that slow beat, beat, beat. I lay on my back and held onto the bear's fur with both hands.

Later, when I woke up, I couldn't remember where I was for a minute, but I could feel Jeremiah lying next to me, breathing loud, asleep.

It was the middle of the night, or maybe real early in the morning. It was still dark, but there was a moon out the window. My eyes started to be able to see the outlines of everything in the room. Jeremiah was still sleeping, but I had to get up.

I slipped back into my underwear and walked all around the house, touching everything, pretending like I belonged here, like these were my silk plants and my wood fruit.

Downstairs, I found the kitchen, and a couple of bedrooms. I imagined all the clothes I would have if I lived in a place like this, all my dresses and shoes and diamonds. I wouldn't bring them here to the cabin, maybe I would leave them in a safe in my closet at home in my real house, or something like that, but I don't know. I never had diamonds. I don't know what diamond people do.

After we got back from the courthouse, Jeremiah's mama opened a jar she kept hidden in the back of her sock drawer and bought us rings for $18 each at Walmart. I wanted to get mine engraved, but that was too much money, so I just stood there and didn't say nothing but thank you to his mama. She didn't like me much, I could tell, but what can you do.

So Jeremiah and I never had a honeymoon, or anything like that. In the middle of the night, while I walked around the cabin, I got the idea that this was our honeymoon. We'd never had anything nice. We deserved it.

I wanted to surprise Jer, maybe make something for him. There were pots and pans in the kitchen, but I couldn't find any food. The fridge was dead empty, not even a bottle of ketchup in there.

The best I could think of was go back upstairs and get dressed again. There were a few dollar bills, so old they'd gone soft, in the back pocket of my jeans.

Instead of sneaking out the window the way we came in, I just walked right out the front door. It was my house. These were my woods.

I walked fast along the path. I was glad I'd brought my jacket. It was so cold outside I could see my breath.

I walked to the store and picked out eggs, and orange soda, and a loaf of day-old bread for 99¢.

It was real early in the morning, but there were a lot of people who couldn't sleep, it seemed, and only one person working, so I stood in line for a long time, looking at magazines and wishing I had enough to buy one, just so I could do something stupid like sit in that house with no books and read about famous people and all their cars and houses and fancy clothes.

There was a clock spinning round on the wall by the customer service this whole time, and when it was her turn, the lady in front of me wanted to pay with a check, but she couldn't find her checkbook in this big old bag she had. She kept taking things out and saying, No, that's not it, things like a tube of lipstick or something we could see perfectly well weren't no checkbook.

But she seemed like a nice lady, kind of old, with round gray curls and a face like a big pincushion, and she said to me, Sorry, like it mattered that I was standing there having to wait, so it gave me a good feeling toward her and I didn't mind waiting while she found a pen and asked who she should make the check out to.

Then it was my turn. I counted out my money, those old limp dollar bills, and watched them go into the pile of ones in the cash drawer.

I was ashamed for a minute, standing in line at the 24-hour grocery at just past 4 o'clock in the morning, thinking what would my mama say if she could see me in my greasy jeans and my old jean jacket, hair not washed in days, but then the clerk handed me a plastic bag and a few coins and

I forgot all that and left the store, heading back in the direction of the cabin.

The door was unlocked so I walked right in, nice as you please, and locked it up again. The eyes in them pictures was still watching me, but they didn't seem so spooky no more. I could see now that they were just watching, paying attention.

When I went upstairs to check on him, Jeremiah was still asleep. I took off my jacket and put it on the table with the wood bowl full of apples. I could hear rain, just starting, on those high windows. I was glad I was back already when that happened. It made me think again that I'm lucky, or we're lucky together. I always feel that way when I'm with him.

The kitchen was at the back most part of the house, far away from the road, so I took a chance and turned on the little light over the stove. The kitchen was real clean and nothing was out on the counters at all. I found a frying pan in one of the cabinets underneath. I wanted to cook eggs the way my stepdaddy showed me. It's funny, I thought. He might be at home, cooking eggs right this second for all I know. If you believe in some kind of a parallel universe, I thought to myself, maybe he's even making breakfast for my old self, right now at the same time I'm standing here, making breakfast for somebody else.

So I was thinking about him the whole time I was frying the bread, frying those eggs, kicking myself for not remembering to look around the store for a pat of butter or some such so the eggs don't stick, never mind that I didn't have enough to pay for it, because these house people don't have even the slightest thing to cook with in this big old kitchen, and wishing we had real juice, and coffee to go in the coffee pot, and then also cream and sugar, but there had to be some limits. They had plates, at least, and forks.

I set the pan to soak and then I went and woke Jeremiah before the food could get cold.

After we ate, it was still dark out and raining even more, and Jeremiah wanted to go back to the bearskin. He wanted to lie there naked again, and go back to sleep after. His hands were already trying to pull me down and unbutton my jeans. He wanted to stay there all day and probably all night besides, but it gave me a jittery feeling to stay in one place too long. I was too scared of getting caught, and it was just something that was always in the back of my brain, if you want to know the truth. I was never not worried about somebody walking in and finding me lying on the floor on their bear rug.

Still, though, I laid my body down with Jeremiah. I did love him, I do, and I wanted to feel him inside me, all around me, holding me close.

It was so peaceful then, with the sound of the rain on the windows, and I don't know when we woke up again. It was daytime but still darkish because of the weather.

I got up and cleaned the kitchen, the forks and plates we'd used. I scrubbed up the pan real good, making sure to get all them nasty burned-on bits washed down the sink. I dried everything with paper towels, and put the paper towels and all the garbage from breakfast in a plastic bag in my backpack. I was planning to throw that bag away somewhere, maybe outside the gas station next time we stopped to buy a box of those little powdered doughnuts.

Soon, I knew we were going to leave again, sneak back out the window with the broken latch, and close it up tight so no one would ever know we'd been inside. I wanted to leave the skin of the house smoothed down, perfect, just the way we found it, with no little scars or stains.

First, though, I took Jeremiah in the bathroom. We hadn't had a real shower in I couldn't remember when. Just a quick wash in the sinks at the public library or at the park before the guy came to lock those bathrooms up for the night. There was no soap in this shower, but then why would they leave it? I brought the dish soap from the kitchen, and it made my hair feel too dry but I didn't care. It was just nice to feel clean for once.

We had to dry off with our dirty clothes, the best parts we could find of them, and then we went back up to the living room and pulled out what we had left in our backpacks, underwear and shirts that I'd washed at the laundry last time we had a few quarters.

Jeremiah said we should've thought of this before, that these people probably had a washer and dryer tucked away somewhere, but now it was too late to look. He looked aggravated because even though I know he wanted to stay, I'd put all these thoughts in his head about leaving. I was just so paranoid about these people coming in and finding us here.

Where we gonna go? he was asking. You know it'll be cold tonight.

I was starting to get the shakes. Jeremiah had already gotten dressed, and I wanted to pull on my clothes, too, but I couldn't make myself do it. I knew we needed to hurry, but I felt so tired all the sudden. I didn't have the energy to do what I needed to do. So instead I lay down and wrapped myself up in the bear's skin. I just wanted to disappear. I was shaking and shaking. My teeth, my muscles—everything ached.

Stop it, Jeremiah said, and I don't know why, but I just couldn't stop. I cried all over that bear's white fur. I could feel it soft against my face, against my arms and legs and back, and I felt like I was the bear, or the bear was me, or some mix of the two, if that makes sense.

All the time I was crying I knew that soon I'd have to get up and put on my clothes and leave this house, but I didn't want our honeymoon to be over yet; I didn't want this to be the end of it. So I lay there as long as I could, trying to remember everything that had happened.

Why you cryin'? Jeremiah asked. His voice was so far away he might as well have been in another room.

I could hear him sigh and unzip his jacket.

Finally I wiped my eyes and let go of the bear's fur and became myself again. I smoothed him out as best I could, and I got my clothes and backpack on, and then Jeremiah and I went out the window of the cabin and back to our own life.

WAX

She bought a Colt .45 and hid it in a carved wooden box under her bed.

There had been times, earlier in her life, when she'd looked forward to the night, the dark dropping like a veil. At the beginning of their marriage, she would sit at work, the last hour, watching the clock. At home, they made dinner, drank a little, went to bed.

Home was an island, then.

Now she dreaded the dark room, the endless hours — the faint light from the television casting mutable shadows against the walls. At some point, she always gave up on sleep and put the television on for company, something light, something with a laugh track, something to obscure the sound of the cars creeping past in the middle of the night. (*Going where, at this hour?*)

All night, she tossed and turned.

And then, very early in the morning, when she had fallen asleep at last, there were the birds, breaking the silence. The squirrels using a tree branch next to her bedroom window as a bridge onto the roof.

She dissolved tablets under her tongue and lay under the covers, looking up at the ceiling.

She wanted a dog. A dog would protect her from . . . what was this?

In the bathtub, she loosened the blade from a razor and ran it lightly against her wrists. *All I have to do is press it,* she thought, but instead she laid it on the side of the tub and leaned back onto the towels she had folded into a makeshift pillow.

She read a short story about a man who had killed himself and gone to some unnamed afterlife where he got a job and went grocery shopping and spent his evenings in bars, drinking and shooting pool. She was filled with horror and dread at the idea of another life after this one filled again with these mundane tasks—with the same traffic and long lines and phone calls and tax forms—the obligations, the illness and boredom and loneliness.

Could this be, she thought—continuous worlds that we walk through like a shotgun apartment or a series of train cars, one leading inexorably to the next?

Before, on her way to the bank, with the zippered deposit bag of cash concealed in a reusable canvas grocery bag, she had almost hoped that she might be hit by a car on her way across the street, or that she would be shot going into or out of the bank, but now it no longer seemed like a cure.

Still, too, she was desperately afraid that the thief would botch the job, and she would wind up in the hospital on life support. Then the police would have to track down her husband in his new condo next to the golf course and bring him in to make medical decisions or identify what was left of her body. Just one more indignity. The cathedral where he had once been a supplicant, now in ruins.

So she returned from the bank and sat back down at her desk. She was so still in the chair that she could have been a piece of moss, a bit of lichen. The numbers on the spreadsheet in front of her grew soft edges and slid across the page—or scampered, rabbit-like, into an ancient forest, across earth and leaves shaded by trees so enormous that she couldn't see their uppermost branches.

But then she blinked and the numbers returned to their cells.

At home she slumped on the couch and watched recordings of reruns of cooking shows—Martha Stewart with her cool efficiency, kindly Jacques Pépin and the tomatoes, the sauces—and she ached for someone who would take care of her.

At work, she had always been the one who organized the party and brought in a card. In the first days, they had said, "I don't know how you can be so calm," and she had shrugged, and it had not been an act. It had been real, but it was also not real. She'd been hollowed out somehow in a way that she could never fully explain, but it didn't matter now; too much time had gone by. She could feel herself shrinking—she was a child, an egg—something another woman could hold in the palm of her hand.

She was in a trance. She walked through the smaller train car of each day on her way to the next life.

She went home and took off her clothes and lay alone in the wreckage that was the bed they used to share.

And then, one morning, she didn't wake until the alarm switched on. She went to work earlier than usual, and when she walked into the building, she found that the hardwood had been waxed overnight. The floor was so shiny that she could see the ceiling lights reflected in it.

She stood there on the periphery, with her coffee cup still warm against her hand, and she looked at the lights, and she felt that maybe it would be possible to go on.

RING

On the subway one night, he noticed a woman in a flowered dress wearing a ring with a deep blue stone as big as a sparrow's egg. She was sitting on an inside seat, alone, staring out the window. It was odd because she had no purse or bags, and unlike the other passengers, she was not listening to headphones or looking at a cellular phone. She didn't have so much as a magazine to look at.

He had been planning to exit at the next stop, but instead he stayed on the train, interested to see where she was going. They were already near the end of the line. It was a nice night, and he didn't have work the next day, so he figured he could just walk home afterward.

At some point, though, he must have looked away or dozed off for a few minutes, because when he turned back, she had disappeared.

A few months went by, then a few years. Eventually, he stopped looking for the woman with the blue ring. By that time, she had packed the dress in a box and moved away. She got a more serious job and stopped wearing the ring, which was really only a pretty piece of costume jewelry. At a certain point, the young woman on the train had begun to live only as a figment of his imagination. And then that, too, ceased to exist.

DOUBLE YOU

I decided to make a list of everything I knew about the Jonathans.

The one in the cubicle to my left had glasses and a comb-over. The one in the house across the street was a bit younger, with smaller glasses and darker hair.

At least, that's what I thought at first.

I was at home one afternoon, a Saturday, reading the newspaper. The Jonathan from work rang my doorbell. I was surprised when I saw who it was. In all these years, it was the first time we had seen each other without our neckties.

"Why are you here?" I said. Or I wanted to say. I could remember no pressing engagement.

Still, we had to work in close proximity. I didn't want to make him angry or uncomfortable. So I said, "Why are you here?" in a more welcoming tone than I might have otherwise.

"Would you like me to mow your lawn?" he asked. A lawnmower was already at the bottom of my front steps, ready to go. Under the comb-over, he was sweating. "I was in the neighborhood."

I walked just over the threshold and looked down the street in either direction. I'm not sure what I was looking for. A getaway car, perhaps?

To imagine where I was, draw two vertical, parallel lines on a piece of paper. The line on the right, the eastern line, should be blue, because it is the river. Use colored pencils if you have them available.

Farther west is the line on the left, the road. The road leads from the center of this tiny town, where our office is situated, and runs directly north: parallel, as I stated earlier, to the river. (You may wish to draw a star or other marker at the bottom of the road, denoting the city center.)

Up to the north, about an inch above the city center and perpendicular to the main road, start drawing several lines, all parallel to each other. Think of a comb, laid on its side, with the teeth heading west. These are the numbered streets.

You should start at the bottom with 1st Street and proceed all the way up to 15th. I myself live at 1525 11th Street North. There are similarly numbered streets below the town that make up its southern end. (If you would like to indicate my house on the 11th Street that is north of town, please do so at this time.)

We should get back to this work Jonathan, though, the one who was standing on my porch. He lived somewhere south of the city; I was sure of it. He had the rumpled clothes and sad demeanor of someone who belonged on the bottom of a map.

"You want to mow my lawn?" I asked. This was not the most bizarre exchange we'd ever had, so I was less incredulous than you might expect.

"I thought you might have been sick," he said. "I mean . . ." He stepped back and gestured at the neighbors' lawns, lingering for what seemed like an inordinate amount of time with his arm in the direction of the across-the-street Jonathan.

Young Jonathan of the dark hair and small glasses just happened to be kneeling outside. If you knew him, you'd know that this was not an unlikely coincidence.

He had a trowel and a pair of hedge-clippers nearby, but at this particular moment, he was painstakingly rearranging the formation of his decorative stones using the fingertips of his gardening gloves.

Unlike my lawn, which had unruly patches of crabgrass, his lawn was a healthy, luxurious green, newly shorn and shining in the sunlight. I often woke, on Saturday mornings, to the sound of his mower.

"If it would make you happy," I said to the work Jonathan, and went back inside the house. This was how I responded to many of his work requests as well, so he was not unused to my calm and agreeable demeanor.

"Obsessed with lawns," I wrote on my list. I had drawn two columns, the one on the left for the first Jonathan (work Jonathan) and the one on the right for the newer version, who had moved in across the street only one year earlier. I added this comment on both sides of the vertical line separating these two columns.

You may have drawn your map of the town on a loose sheet of paper, and that is not a problem. You may continue to work using this method.

However, if you decide to make your own copy of my list about the Jonathans, etc., then it may be simpler to collect all of your materials in one place. If you don't already have one, you might want to consider investing in a good notebook for this purpose.

So I added the comment about the lawns to my list, and I went back to the newspaper. As you can imagine, it was difficult to concentrate with the noise of the mower in the background. I finally had to get up and go into the back room to avoid the one Jonathan sweating back and forth past my picture window and the other arranging stones as though his life depended on it.

At work on Monday, the cubicle Jonathan came to speak to me. He didn't mention the weekend. Had I finished my paperwork: that is what he wanted to talk about now.

Up close, as he was speaking, I couldn't help noticing that his teeth protruded a bit from his upper lip, and it was difficult for him to close his mouth all the way. Is there a name for that? I felt certain that a dentist would have a strong, scientific-sounding term for it.

(In your notebook, perhaps you should make a list of words. Add "maxillary prognathism" as a starting point for your research.)

It was strange, though, about his teeth. I had never noticed this before.

When I got home, Jonathan (neighbor Jonathan) was dragging his trash bin out to the curb. The trash would not be collected for another 12.5 hours by my calculations, but darned if that man wasn't on top of things.

"Howdy!" he said. (Howdy?) "Would you like me to bring out your trash?"

Now, I am not as young and virile as I once was. But I am somewhere between the two Jonathans in age, and I've kept reasonably fit, if I do say so myself. The bin is on wheels, for goodness' sake!

"I thought there might be something wrong," he added, seeming to understand that he might have committed a faux pas. "You know, since you stopped mowing your lawn."

The lawn again!

I itched to write something down, but I'd already written "obsessed with lawns" in my notebook. That had seemed thorough enough at the time. Now it was just begging for an asterisk or two.

Something about this neighbor Jonathan seemed familiar. It was the teeth again. Things balanced out better on his face, but there was a faint similarity.

The more I looked around, the more everything seemed out of place.

"Whose car is that in your driveway?" I asked suspiciously.

Jonathan took a long time turning around and looking. He shrugged. "I have a new roommate."

"If you say so."

He seemed surprised by this. "Well, nice seeing you," he said.

I watched him walk back to his yard. He paused over the flower beds, tucking stray leaves and petals back in order. When he went inside, the yard looked so perfect it might have been made out of plastic.

~

29 June. 8:03 a.m.

Leaving my house when I saw W.J. leaving the neighbor's house across the street. (Is it possible that his hair is growing in a little bit? Can balding be reversed?)

Work Jonathan: Well, fancy meeting you here! (Awkward laugh.)

Me: Why would I be meeting you?

Jonathan: Wait, no. I didn't . . . I just meant that we'll probably be seeing a lot of each other now that I moved in with Jonathan.

Me: What?

Jonathan: We met when I was mowing your lawn.

Me: My lawn?

Jonathan: Maybe we should start carpooling.

~

All the way to work I replayed this scene in my mind.

The Jonathan from work met the gardening Jonathan and struck up a friendship, and now we are all neighbors. This explanation struck me as odd.

I sat in the parking lot until I saw the work Jonathan go inside the building. We were both early, so I could afford a few minutes to let him get settled and immersed in his paperwork. When I was sure enough time had elapsed, I could duck inside.

Oblivious as ever, Jonathan seemed unaware that I was avoiding him. Just before lunch, he popped his head into my cubicle.

"Would you like a sandwich from the deli? My treat." He was smiling and I could see those teeth again.

Had he had them first, or the other Jonathan? I could no longer remember. They seemed to be morphing into the same person.

One of them wanted to buy me a sandwich. One of them wanted to take out his trash far too early. When I got home, they were both standing in the driveway across the street. They stood next to each other, watching as I got out of my car.

Hadn't one of them been taller before? The work one had definitely slimmed down in some way. His little pot belly was almost gone. They both had the same glasses and a faint five-o'clock shadow. It had gotten to a point where I was having trouble telling them apart.

I had stopped at the store on the way home, and they penned me in as I was pulling a heavy bag out of the car.

They were bantering back and forth, and one said lightly, "You're the only person who's ever said that to me." Their voices had even changed, both deeper and with a more pronounced Minnesota accent.

The one that I thought was work Jonathan didn't have his sad look anymore. I decided to make a note of that when I got inside.

"Do you need any help?" the neighbor asked.

"I like to do things myself," I said.

As if he hadn't heard, he said, "We should have you over this weekend."

"That's a great idea," his sidekick chimed in.

They both looked at me owlishly, their big eyes unblinking behind their glasses.

One of them was wearing a necktie that matched my own. "You're practically a Jonathan," he said, pointing, and the other one laughed.

Startled, I said, "I'm not a Jonathan!"

The laughing one sobered up right away. "Of course not," he amended. He tipped his head to one side, considering. "It's so strange, though," he said. "You've always reminded me of someone I know."

The other Jonathan nodded. They both studied me as though I were some kind of unusual botanical specimen.

"Well, I should get inside," I said.

I shouldered past them and unlocked the front door of my house. I could hear their chitchat behind me, growing fainter as they walked back across the street.

When I was safely inside, I set down my bags and locked the door. I peeked through the curtains in my living room. They were still outside, just a couple of nondescript middle-aged men with dark hair and glasses, pulling on their gardening gloves and getting to work.

JEOPARDY

Around the corner from her aunt's house, there's a strip mall with a little Chinese bakery, a nail salon, and a 7-Eleven. That's the only place within walking distance that's open at midnight, when her aunt mutes the TV and says she wants a donut and a pack of cigarettes.

Sometimes Sophie has work the next morning and is already in bed asleep, but tonight she's awake, sitting under an afghan on the living room couch. The cat is curled up next to her, licking her paws.

"It's cold out," Sophie says, hoping that this will end the conversation, though she knows that it won't.

Her aunt only smokes out on the back porch; she's down to two cigarettes a day, one after lunch and one after dinner, but sometimes she has what she calls a little slip-up.

"I don't mind," her aunt says. "It's stuffy in here anyway. I could use a breath of fresh air." She adds, "When you go, you can borrow my jacket."

Later, Sophie will wonder how things might have been different if she had said no, or tried to wheedle out of it for a bit longer. Five, ten minutes, even.

But she doesn't.

She takes the money and walks around the corner to the strip mall. The shop where she works is in a different part of town and has big wooden buckets of pansies outside. Here there are cigarette butts and a glass bottle that someone set down on the sidewalk.

A man is standing with his back to her; she can't see any part of his face, just a long black trench coat and a porkpie hat. She has walked into the 7-Eleven and is standing in front of the donuts when the image of that coat comes back to her, but by then it's too late: he's already inside, waving a gun at the cashier. Yelling.

Sophie remembers something from her childhood, a yelling man, a scene. Her mother stepping in front of her, protecting her from whatever was happening. That was a different store, though, a different time.

She accidentally knocks a box off the shelf and the man turns, startled. "Don't move!" he shouts.

They are all in the wrong place at the wrong time. The words beat loudly in her head. Wrong place, wrong time. Wrong place, wrong time.

Somehow, she needs to call for help, but her cell phone is back at her aunt's house, lying on the coffee table. She was just walking around the corner.

Her aunt won't know what happened to her. At least she is wearing Jason's old sweatshirt, the one he left behind when he moved out of their apartment. If she has to die, at least she can die in the sweatshirt.

(*Will he find out?* she wonders. Is that a detail that would make it into the paper? Woman found shot to death in comfortably worn UT sweatshirt?)

On TV, it's the final round. The category is Movies & The Bible. Alex says, "In this crime drama, a 1994 Oscar nominee for Best Picture, a character misquotes Ezekiel 25:17 twice."

The contestants frown and look down at their boards.

When the music stops, it turns out that the guy in third place, the one with the beard and the kind eyes, is the only one who has written "What is *Pulp Fiction*?" on his board. He looks as surprised as anyone when he almost doubles his score and wins the game.

Sophie's aunt mutes the TV. She wants a bag of chips, a diet Dr Pepper, and a pack of cigarettes. Maybe an apple, too, she says thoughtfully.

The local news has already started. Sophie is staring at the television. The cat is on her lap.

For just a second, she can't remember. Is this the memory? Or is this what is happening now, here, tonight? She can see the cigarettes on the shelves behind the cash register. She has to walk past the gunman to get to them. She has to call for help.

Her cell phone is at her aunt's house. Jason is gone. The cashier is on the floor. It's too late.

"Yes," her aunt says. "Definitely an apple." She looks at Sophie. "Do you feel well enough to go?"

Sophie left work an hour early because of a stress headache. "I'm fine," she says, ignoring the usual pinch of fear. "I can go."

Her aunt hands her a crumpled twenty-dollar bill, saying no, she forgot. Don't get the cigarettes.

Sophie walks around the corner. The front doors of the nail salon are propped open, and she can smell chemicals and nail polish. It's summer again, evening, but the days are long enough that it's still light out.

Inside the store, she picks out the apple, a liter of soda, and a bag of chips. She offers the twenty and doesn't ask this cashier for anything that's held behind the counter. Her aunt hasn't smoked in two days. She promised; this time, she was quitting for good.

When Sophie gets back to the house, though, her aunt has been out on the porch. Even from across the room, Sophie can smell it on her.

Her aunt sits in her chair, staring at the screen. She doesn't look up, not even when Sophie puts the plastic bag and the change on the TV tray next her plate.

It's been a long time since her aunt agreed to let her stay in the spare bedroom for a couple of weeks while Sophie found a new apartment. By now, anyone else would have left a newspaper on the dining room table with the ads for rentals circled in red.

So she says nothing—turning, instead, to pick up the cat. Her aunt opens the bag of chips without taking her eyes off the television.

On the news, two surfers are receiving an award for bravery. A month earlier, they attempted to rescue two teenage brothers who ran into a ten-foot swell and were pulled out to sea by a strong rip current. The younger brother was saved. The older brother drowned.

There were hundreds of people on the beach that day, the newscaster says. Other surfers in the water, a wedding party on the shore.

This segues into the weather, delivered by a cheerful man in a three-piece suit. He looks toward the map beside him, pointing at temperatures. The weekly forecast is a mixed bag: some days are marked with a cloud, others with a bright yellow sun ringed by triangular orange points for rays.

Sophie is looking for more meaningful guidance, but the weatherman's blank smile gives nothing away. He never says whether these will be days of remembering, or days of forgetting. He doesn't look through the screen and predict which person watching will be the unlucky brother on any given day.

During the commercial, her aunt cracks open the soda and takes a quick, surreptitious drink. Sophie gets comfortable on the couch again. The cat is lying on her stomach. A woman on television vacuums her carpet, back and forth, then scrutinizes the results. She turns toward the viewer with a helpless expression. And even though Sophie has seen this play out a hundred times before, she leans forward a little, waiting to see what happens next.

WHITE FLAG

She wanted to be like Elizabeth Taylor in *Butterfield 8*, beautiful and world-weary, but it seemed that Elizabeth Taylor in *Who's Afraid of Virginia Woolf?* was more her style: half in the bag and walking around the kitchen late at night eating a cold chicken leg with the refrigerator door hanging open. She, too, had gained weight for the role of a lifetime, and her husband, like Richard Burton, was bitter and past his prime. They continuously circled each other, competing for the upper hand.

It was a mistake, she'd always thought, to marry someone from the same department. They'd both been tenure-track when they met, but they'd gotten full professorships a year apart, and it had almost destroyed their marriage. Still, they'd powered through. Now they lived in a gorgeous red-brick townhouse with bay windows, an enviable record collection, and a pair of chocolate sable standard poodles called Faust and Tosca.

It was late fall, when the outstretched arms of the trees were bleak and naked and the wind was audible even indoors. Leslie had been languishing at home all night, nursing a cold, while Lionel spent the evening at the university, carting around a guest lecturer from Bucharest whom they'd managed to coax out of Romania. Leslie was furious. It had been her idea to invite him in the first place, and it had taken months to get Lionel on board. She was the one who'd made the phone calls, written the letters, gotten the funding. All so she could spend the evening holed up in bed with a box of tissues and a book she felt too sick to read.

The doorbell rang. The dogs careened from the bedroom as if they'd been shot out of a cannon. Lionel must have forgotten his keys again.

Leslie sighed, a long-suffering sigh. She left her wineglass on the bedside table and took her time getting up. Let him wait.

The dogs were at the door, quivering, barking like maniacs. Lionel had promised to train them, or at least to have them trained, but he never had. He was out on the front porch, champagne bottle in hand.

The Romanian scholar had been taken out for drinks and deposited safely back in his hotel room, but Lionel wasn't ready to call it a night. He'd brought home a pair of graduate students he'd taken on a study trip to London the previous spring. He introduced them with his free hand: Lithe Something and Tall and Gorgeous Somethingelse. They were both in their twenties and wearing short, tight dresses that showed off their long legs and impressive cleavage, and when faced with their professor's wife at home in her pajamas, they at least had the decency to look sheepish, even if Lionel didn't.

Lionel sat the students down on the couch and disappeared into the kitchen, and Leslie put on a record to cover the silence. Before they knew it, he was back with champagne flutes and a box of water crackers. He pushed the magazines fanned across the coffee table out of the way and set everything down. Leslie was the one who always roasted the figs and arranged the cheese board, so she wasn't surprised. Without her, Lionel was utterly helpless. She perched on the arm of a chair and shook her head, amused. He hadn't even remembered a plate.

No matter. He removed the foil from the champagne bottle and tossed it aside. The dogs batted it across the floor. He eased off the wire cage and theatrically popped the cork, making the girls squeal. Champagne foamed out onto his hand and across a copy of *Architectural Digest* before he could reach the glasses. He'd had too much to drink already, Leslie could tell, but he was handing out flutes of champagne one second and going back to the kitchen for a bottle of Riesling the next. He was nothing if not an overachiever.

This time, at least, he brought back a corkscrew. "Are you the single mom?" Leslie asked one of the girls. "Or are you the one who's pregnant now?"

She was only asking to be mean, but the taller girl said, "Janell is the one who's pregnant. She couldn't make it tonight. I'm the mom." She looked pleased, as if Leslie's questions meant that Lionel had singled her out. This somehow made it worse. The girl pulled a cell phone out of her bra and started scrolling through photos of her little boy, angling the phone so that Leslie and the other girl could see.

Leslie didn't get up from the arm of the chair. Her cold medicine had finally kicked in, but she pulled a tissue out of her pajama pocket and dabbed her nose delicately. "I shouldn't get too close," she said.

"Don't mind her," Lionel said to the girls. "She's not really sick. She just likes the attention." He poured each girl a glass of wine and sat down on the couch in between them.

"That's absurd," Leslie said. She raised her hand and turned it over to reveal the ball of tissue in her palm. A magic trick. Evidence.

The single mom tucked the phone back against her breast and took a sip of wine.

Lionel leaned back against the couch. "Would you like to see my first editions?" he asked—his idea of a come-on—and Leslie narrowed her eyes. Neither girl took the bait.

"They don't care about that," Leslie said. "Look." She whistled, and the dogs did a trick. Dutifully, the girls clapped. Faust and Tosca returned to their posts next to the couch, bookending Lionel and his devotees.

From the kitchen, the tea kettle whistled. Leslie rose hospitably and brought back glasses filled with ice cubes and tea bags and arranged them in a circle on the coffee table. When she tipped the kettle each time, the water was so hot that the ice cracked in the glass.

The record wound down, and Leslie didn't replace it. She sipped her drink, relishing the silence.

One of the girls asked to use the restroom. She walked down the dark hallway and left Lionel sitting next to the tall girl with the little boy at home.

"Hello, Mother," Leslie said from her perch on the arm of the chair. She leaned toward the couch, and Lionel and the tall girl shrank back a little. Leslie felt woozy from the combination of cold medicine and too much wine. She sank into the empty spot next to the tall girl, pushing them both over a little.

The tall girl, caught in between, blushed. From the other side of the couch, Lionel shifted, putting his hand on her knee.

He bent toward the girl, breathing what Leslie knew was his hot, boozy breath onto her, pretending that he was merely accentuating a point. He squeezed her leg emphatically.

Leslie leaned in as well, smiling, and put her hand on the girl's other knee. "Isn't he bright?" she asked. "I've always thought so."

The girl leapt to her feet, pulling down the hem of her dress. She stammered as she made an excuse and fled. Hastily, on her way out the door, she whipped her coat from the hall closet. It took a moment for the empty hangers to stopped clicking against each other.

"Well, bless her heart," Leslie said. She shrugged and drank more of her tea. It wasn't the first time this had happened, and it wouldn't be the last.

When the other girl emerged from the restroom, Leslie offered to drive her home. The buzz from the wine had worn off, and she was no longer enjoying herself. She left Lionel to entertain this one while she went into the bedroom and stripped off her pajamas. At the university, she was famous for her clothes: every day last semester, she had worn vintage party dresses and heels.

On her teaching evaluations, a student had written, "I can always hear her coming."

She put on a coat of lipstick and brushed her hair.

They were already waiting at the front door when Leslie returned. The girl looked startled, unhappy, and she stood meekly as Lionel retrieved first his coat, then both of theirs.

Leslie took her time with the buttons and smoothed her hair over the collar. "Ready?" Lionel asked. He twirled a ring of keys around his finger.

They took their places in the car, with Lionel and Leslie in front and the girl buckled in the back seat as if she were their child. Lionel started out strong but then he grazed a mailbox and lost his momentum. He was the ice skater who falls in competition and can't quite regain his confidence. He hit another mailbox, then a tree.

"Just a minute, now," Lionel said, but the girl already had her door open. She was halfway out of the car when he threw it into reverse and tapped the gas. The girl fell onto the grass. Lionel braked. "Are you all right?" he asked, easy as you please, but the girl didn't answer—she was limping and in heels, but still, she ran away as best she could, a wounded deer.

"Well, you've lost another student," Leslie said. Lionel didn't answer. He wasn't interested in learning any lessons.

The wind blew against the windows of the car. Leaves swirled around them. Leslie unbuckled her seatbelt and got out to close the girl's door again. When she returned to her seat, they backed away from the tree and drove home.

Lionel unlocked the front door. Inside, the dogs were on their cushions, and they raised their heads but didn't get up.

The lights were still blazing in the living room. Lionel surveyed the wreckage. "We should open another bottle of wine," he said. "What do you think?"

It was late, and Leslie had grown weary of playing Elizabeth Taylor. She wasn't in the mood, tonight, to lose her mind or drive off a cliff.

Coyly, she turned the pockets of her coat inside out to show him that they were empty: no tricks. She tucked them back in and then produced from the empty pockets two clean white tissues. She waved them in his direction like flags.

Lionel shook his head, bored. He parodied a mocking clap. But then, at last, he surrendered, too. He sighed and rolled his eyes and kissed her, and turned off the living room lights and took her to bed.

THE VIRTUOSO (CIRCA 2018)

The pianist strides onto the stage in a long, form-fitting silver column dress, its sequins catching the light as she bows to the audience. Behind her, the orchestra members are in their seats, fanned out in a half circle. She arranges herself on the piano bench, smoothing her dress and placing her hands in her lap as the conductor raises his baton, the violinists and flautists silently lifting their instruments, and with a fluid movement from the conductor, the piece begins.

Until her solo, the pianist remains seated, moving almost imperceptibly in time with the orchestra, entranced, until there is a lull in the music and the piano enters it, the woman's hands flowing over the keys as if through water: glimmering, effortless. She plays without sheet music, as if the notes have been absorbed into her body. The concerto is alternately a bright and sparkling river, with its various twists and turns, and an ocean roiling and coming to rest.

When she plays the last note of the third movement, there is a long pause, her fingers hovering over the keys before landing in her lap again.

The conductor's baton remains frozen in place, and the audience remains motionless as the stage lights darken and a spotlight frames the pianist. She rises from the piano bench and faces the audience, raising her arms as everyone watches in silence, and strips off her dress, revealing a wrestler's singlet, also silver and dazzling with sequins.

A second spotlight illuminates a single chair placed to the side of the stage. A woman in a tight pink mini-dress rises and walks toward the piano.

The two women meet center-stage and face each other, bowing before circling each other predatorily like cats. In the room is hushed anticipation. The pianist strikes first, punching the other woman in the face so hard that her head snaps back, and the woman in pink never quite recovers; the pianist beats her down to the ground and doesn't rest until she stops twitching.

As the second spotlight dims, leaving the crumpled pink dress in darkness, the pianist raises her arms above her head in a wide, triumphant V. Her face is glowing. The conductor brings down his baton and turns, signaling the end of the composition, and the audience erupts into frantic applause.

HOPE FOR THE FUTURE

[She] loved to close her eyes and put the shell to her ear—from those monstrous, salmon-colored jaws you could hear the call of a faraway country, so far away that a place could no longer be found for it on the globe . . .
—Tatyana Tolstaya, "Fire and Dust,"
from her book *White Walls*

On the street, cars passed by in a haze of noise and exhaust, the taxi drivers stamping on their brakes and jerking the wheel to whip past whoever was slowing them down—once, on a street too clogged to complete this maneuver, a motorcyclist had lost his helmet in the road and had stopped, briefly, to retrieve it, blocking the lane by hopping down and taking a few steps back while the taxi driver behind him, enraged, leaned violently on his horn, and there was no pity for anyone, they had ceased to exist as such, they were only obstacles. In an expensive city, they were thieves, robbing everyone around them of precious time and money.

She took the side streets, which were no better, and sidestepped broken bottles and bags of trash, and for a while, an old moth-eaten couch, worn through so deeply in places that the springs were exposed, but then another day a woman was sitting delicately on one side of it with her hands in her lap as if she were waiting for a bus—and as she walked by the woman reached toward her, almost grazing her clothes with these fingers, these cracked and broken nails, or it might have been another day, when a woman sitting in a blanket nest on the sidewalk smiled and asked if she had a brother, and that woman was wearing a tiara crusted with rhinestones and nearby on the pavement was a clear plastic jug filled with something that looked like urine, and it had been there for days with its darkening liquid until—like the couch and the women and the hand reaching toward her—it suddenly disappeared.

There was a time—in childhood, perhaps—when she'd gone to the ocean, though that too could have been a dream—her father had been dead for many years, and there was no one left to ask—but she remembered the large, old-fashioned metal key, warming in her hand, and the floor of the motel room, gritty with sand she'd tracked inside after a long day out in the sun, and while the ocean waves lapped softly at the shore, a warm wind billowed the white tulle at the open window, but that really was a dream, or something she'd read in a book, and bore no resemblance to the water that slid past her current city—hostile, torpid, discolored by chemicals, lying in wait, threatening with every storm to rage past its oily banks.

The light turned red and she paused on the curb, at the opening between the city blocks, where one towering building stopped and allowed, briefly, a view of a steep cross street leading down to the water, but she waited for the signal and followed the crosswalk to the next gray corner and slipped through the glass doors into the chilled air of the market, keeping her arms close to her body to avoid colliding with other shoppers, mindlessly pushing their carts into her hips as they stared down at their phones, and then she was out on the street again, disgorged by that gaping glass mouth, with the straps of the bags cutting into her shoulders and wrists, and past an alley, the smell of urine again, hanging on the breeze, and the more pleasant smells from a nearby restaurant, and she fumbled with the bags as she extracted her key ring and let herself into the building, and managed the stairs, which seemed so different at the start of the day, on the way down, than they did now, but she shifted her arms and went up a little at a time, and at last was at the door, and as she wrestled it open, she could hear from inside the apartment the telephone ringing, and she had barely closed the door, the keys were still in her hand, but she rushed forward, knocking her leg against the end table in her haste, and answered.

IN THE AIR

She was flying home from Guadalajara when she thought of a man she used to date. He'd been an air traffic controller in El Paso. One night, he had invited her to visit him at work. She climbed the stairs to the top of the tower. All the way around the room, every wall was a window. Outside, it was dark, and to the south, she could see the lights of Juarez.

Standing there, looking across the border into Mexico, Sylvia had the idea that he was going to propose. She had never gotten along with his mother. There were other reasons, too, but this was the first one she thought of. She made an excuse and left, and not long after, she broke things off.

Two years later, Sylvia met her first husband, Michael, at a party in Washington, D.C. He was an American journalist who worked as a foreign correspondent for the Associated Press. He had just returned from a posting in Beijing. They got married and moved overseas. She lost touch with her air traffic controller.

Many years passed. Sylvia and Michael divorced. She returned to the United States. Her parents were still living in Dallas, and she moved in with them until she could decide what to do. One night, after they went to bed, Sylvia drank two glasses of wine and called the old number. She still knew it after all that time. She wasn't sure what she would say if he answered, but the phone just rang and rang.

In the morning, she knew it had been a mistake. Being back in Texas had made her think of him. And then, too, she was just so desperately lonely.

She returned to her research, bought a two-bedroom bungalow with a fenced yard, and got a dog. Sometimes, as she stood at the kitchen counter preparing dinner, she heard noises outside. It was wintertime, dark already. The dog sat on the floor near her, its ears turning to follow the sound. Sometimes the dog went to another room, peered out the window, then returned to her side. Sylvia placed her hand on the dog's back.

At the grocery store, she ran into an old friend, someone Sylvia had known when she lived in El Paso. He had also moved to Dallas. He told her that her ex-boyfriend had been killed in a motorcycle accident a few years earlier. He had just turned forty years old.

The news was hard to absorb. Sylvia had rarely thought of him. Yet she had to admit that at certain low points in her life—after the divorce, for example—it had been a small comfort. She had always nurtured a vague fantasy about his intentions toward her, though by all appearances at the time he'd let her go easily and without regret.

Sylvia thought about writing his mother a letter. So much time had passed, though, and then she could never decide what to say. What was there to say? When her old friend had brought up the ex-boyfriend, it had taken her a second even to remember his last name. Every day when she sat down at her desk, she saw the note she had written to remind herself to write the letter, but instead of getting out a piece of stationary and a pen, she looked at the note and felt guilty. Finally, she threw it away.

She became resigned to middle age. She fell into a routine. Then, at an otherwise tedious university lecture, she met Robert. He was a lawyer at the end of his career. His wife had died of ovarian cancer. They had two grown daughters. Young, but grown.

All of Sylvia's friends said it would be awful. The evil stepmother, the whole trope. Some of them had been through it, one more than once. Sylvia didn't care. She fell headlong into his life. She met his dog and went with him to parties. She let him meet her dog and took him antique shopping on Sundays. Finally, in summer, he had a picnic and introduced her to his girls. Sylvia brought lemon squares dusted with powdered sugar and smiled a lot. The girls were smart and funny, like Robert. She moved in with him and rented out her house. That winter, he took her to his cabin in Aspen and they made love in front of a fire.

They had a small wedding at the arboretum against a backdrop of crape myrtle trees. They traveled. One of Robert's daughters got engaged to a Jewish man, and she asked Sylvia and Robert to stand on either side and walk her down the aisle. Sylvia continued to work at the laboratory. She took up gardening. She developed arthritis in her hands. She became—against all odds, against all logic—a grandmother.

Sylvia flew to Guadalajara for a conference. The morning of her presentation, Robert called her long-distance. Back in Dallas, her mother had fallen getting out of the bathtub. Her left hip was broken. They were scheduled to meet that afternoon with a surgeon. For some time, both of Sylvia's parents had been in ill health. They were both in their late eighties and reeling after a lifetime of excess.

It was possible to change the return flight, though she couldn't leave until early evening. So that was that. Sylvia took her suitcase with her to the auditorium. She walked up to the stage at the front of the room and presented the findings of her research, even answering questions, her mind sharp and focused. As she left the building, though, she shed her resolve: it fell away from her like leaves as she walked away from science and into real life again.

On the plane, she had a window seat. She closed the shade before the plane took off. Somewhere behind her, a child was crying. In the aisle, a flight attendant lifted an emergency oxygen mask and demonstrated how to attach it to her face. She pulled the elastic band toward the back of her head, not bothering to complete the motion. Sylvia closed her eyes. She didn't think it would be possible to sleep, given the circumstances, but when she became aware of an announcement over the loudspeaker, the plane was already at altitude.

Ladies and gentlemen, we are experiencing turbulence, someone said. It was overhead, a disembodied male voice. *Señoras y señores, estamos experimentando turbulencias.* Sylvia shifted uncomfortably. The other passengers seemed unfazed by the announcement. Though the seatbelt sign was illuminated, a woman rose from her seat, lurching down the aisle toward the bathroom.

The airplane jerked from side to side. Sylvia thought uneasily of the vomit bag in the seat pocket in front of her. She closed her eyes, then opened them again. She was going to be ill; she was sure of it. Then, no: the plane righted itself. Her stomach fell back to earth.

She opened the window shade and looked outside. There was nothing there but darkness and clouds. Still, she thought that in the distance, she could see stars, or the patchwork of land below. Time compressed. She was on a pile of quilts in front of a fire, making love to Robert. She was standing in a kitchen with her hand on her dog's back, on his head. Her old dog, long dead now. She was climbing the stairs of an air traffic control tower, holding on to the railing. She was so young, then, and careful. She had no idea that she was on the verge. She walked to the edge of the room and stood at the window, looking out into the night, with the past behind her, and the lights of a distant city laid out at her feet.

SCENTS

Even after she died, there were certain smells that still made Jeanette recoil. A person's scalp after a few days without a shower. A room with a bedpan.

She had worked in a nursing home for many years. She quit when her own mother became ill.

Jeanette converted the dining room of her house into a bedroom. It was the only semi-private room on the first floor, and stairs had become impossible. Jeanette rented a hospital bed from a medical supply company.

This is an ugly story.

Life is full of ugly stories. You might as well get used to it.

It's raining right now.

The sky is gray, or would be if it weren't dark already. It's been gray all day—the rain slopping down outside—just outside the windows of the dining room where Jeanette's mother lived during the last months of her life. (Or years. These things have a way of dragging on.)

Jeanette was a good daughter.

A dutiful daughter.

So, the smell of rain. After her mother died, Jeanette got sick. She spent several months in and out of the hospital. One morning, she was on her way outside, and she was feeling OK. Hurt, fragile, but OK—and even though it was a rainy, dreary day, she was happy to be breathing fresh air for the first time in a few days. She wanted to go home, to take a shower and wash her hair, put on clean clothes—to sit in her armchair with a cup of hot cocoa and a warm blanket.

The orderly pushed her wheelchair outside. There was the smell of the rain. (The smell of the chocolate, the warm fabric.)

Even after she died, she could still remember them.

SENSE

Jeanette's adopted sister had been shaken as a baby and lost her sight. Although she was blind, people always said she had more sense than both her brothers put together.

People said? Their mother said.

She never had anything good to say about the boys. Frick and Frack, she used to call them, with derision.

Jeanette was the youngest, born long after her mother was told she would never have another biological child. Jeanette was a good-natured baby with big blue eyes and dimples. Aren't you lucky, everyone said.

Everyone? Yes, everyone. The doctor, Aunt Ethel, the neighbors.

By the time Jeanette was born, though, her mother had fallen too deeply in love with the blind girl—this exceptional blind girl—and no one else could measure up. (And also, it should be said, she was in love with herself. She loved being the mother of the blind girl.)

This girl could quote an enormous number of things from memory and do complicated math problems in her head. Aren't you lucky, everyone said. To be related to the blind girl.

When Jeanette was still quite young, the blind girl drowned in a pond behind the house. No one called them lucky anymore, and her mother's reign over the family abruptly ended. For more than a year, she drank too much and spent most mornings in bed.

That summer, when she was bored, Jeanette sometimes tiptoed in and walked around the room, looking at her mother's bells and figurines. Her father had mostly stopped coming home, and the maid left at two.

Jeanette froze when her mother opened her eyes. Why are you in here? her mother asked.

There's no more milk.

Ask those good-for-nothings, Frick and Frack, her mother said, but all the venom had gone out of her.

CENTS

After her mother's death, Jeanette retrieved the table and chairs from the garage and moved them back into her dining room. She set up her typewriter at one end of the table, with a ream of paper and a cup full of pens and pencils, facing the window.

The morning sun shone in.

This was in the months before her diagnosis, when she just thought she'd let herself get run down.

She didn't have the energy, yet, to return to work, so she decided to write letters. It seemed important to say what she needed to say. Upstairs were the address book, the envelopes and stamps.

In the hospital, when she decided to refuse the radiation, one of the doctors said, Do you want my two cents?

I'll just take one, Jeanette said, if you don't mind. Two is usually too many.

The doctor smiled. Touché.

In life, Jeanette sat at the typewriter and looked outside. Sometimes she typed, but most of the time, she sat with her fingers laced on the table in front of her and stared mindlessly at the swimming pool surrounded by flowers. This view. The trees, the sky. These had been the last things her mother ever saw in this world.

The doctor touched her hand. Jeanette, exhausted, lying in a hospital bed, felt a spark of attraction between them. That hand on her hand, the briefest moment of contact—but she was reminded in that instant that she was still a living being. Skin, nerve endings. It was a shock to feel desire, again, after all that time.

In another life, she might have been strong and healthy and filled with longing; they might have kissed; the doctor might have lain on top of her and unbuttoned her blouse.

She remembered this, too, after her death—the feeling of lying under another person, and she thought of it often as she lay on her back in the swimming pool, under the clear blue sky, with the sun overhead. If she had risen from the water and walked toward her old house she might have seen through the window a typewriter on a dining room table, or any number of things, but there was nothing there for her any longer, and so instead she closed her eyes and returned to dreaming.

BRUTE

He was the type of person who was always getting into bar fights. It was an easy way to get rid of some aggressive energy, and there was often an explanation that let him come out looking like a good guy. He'd been defending someone's honor, let's say. Every time you ran into him, it seemed, his knuckles were taped.

He and his roommates lived in an apartment building just down the street from a fire station. In that city, firefighters were first responders at everything from highway collisions to your garden-variety home accidents. Day and night, the garage door rolled up and sirens began to scream.

Why don't you move, I asked, and he just shrugged. I didn't push the issue. If you must know, I had discovered that he was an adrenaline junkie in all the ways that mattered. He pulled my hair, clung to the headboard, did everything but hang upside-down as sirens oscillated outside, growing louder and louder, and the engines roared past the open windows.

DARK HORSE

She grew up in New Brunswick, in a small house a few streets down from the thrift store and The Painted Pony Bar and Grill. Her dad was dead, but she had his old record player and a life-sized poster of Jim Morrison hanging on the wall above her bed, and she used to lie on her back and listen to Jimi Hendrix and The Doors and think about William Blake, and the known and the unknown.

The house. While she'd been gone, her mother had hung a sign with the word "Family" on the living room wall, above a series of framed photos. Outside the kitchen window, there was a red barn. Three black cats lived in the hayloft, emerging to eat scraps that her mother left in a bowl by the back door. When the weather was nice, they sat in the setting sun and licked their paws.

She watched them from the window. It was early enough still. She was used to having a cigarette before dinner, and she was trying anything she could to keep her mind elsewhere. She sat in the window seat. She wore a tank top with a long silver chain and a silver cross that touched the top of her cleavage. She had a tattoo arching above her left breast that said "Always in my ♥" in a beautiful script. Sumptuous, her ex had said the first time he saw it, the first time she took her shirt off in front of him.

She had dressed more conservatively then. She'd worked two jobs to put him through school, and then he left her, and what did she have to show for it? They had never even gotten married. Cow/milk, as her grandmother would have said. Shorthand for what they were all thinking. Her mother had worked two jobs, too, but she'd put herself through school instead.

There was a jigsaw puzzle, half-finished on the coffee table. Multicolored rabbits, lined up in a row. She glanced at the picture on the front of the box. The grass in the background would be the killer.

As soon as her mother had left that morning, she'd gone through the cabinets, but her mother had cleaned the place out. There was only, in one of the highest cabinets, a small bottle of ice wine—something she must have received as a gift. They'd always been beer-drinkers, themselves.

Outside, a car pulled up, and she would have expected the cats to scatter, but they held their ground, just as bold as you please. If she hurried, she could get to Moncton and back before her mother got home from work. Through the window, you can see her open the car door and slide into the passenger seat.

She is twenty-seven years old. She's supposed to be waiting around until her uncle gets back from a meeting in Ottawa in a few days so she can ask him for a job at one of his gas stations. She's already been fired twice in the past six months, once for being short with a customer and once for snorting coke in the washroom. That was just for fun, though: something to break up the monotony. She was living in Ontario at the time, and she was cutting the lines with her health card.

The car backs out of the driveway. She is a rabbit herself now, escaping from the hat.

Earlier in the day, she stood at the kitchen sink, filling a glass of water. As she stepped back, for some reason, she dropped the glass. Maybe her hands were wet, or maybe she just forgot that she was holding it. Who knew? She spent a long time on her knees, wiping up the water, picking chips of glass up off the floor.

In the evening, her mother picks her son up from day care and drives home. It's Friday night, dusk. The mother drives past the thrift store and the Painted Pony. Cars are pulling in and out of the parking lot. Behind her, in the back seat, the little boy is talking. That weekend, she wants to make him a good meal, with fruit and a piece of chicken and a big bowl of strawberry shortcake for dessert.

It isn't clear, from the street, whether anyone is inside the house. There is no light from the front window.

The known, the unknown.

Her mother opens the door. From the back bedroom, she can hear Jim Morrison singing "Moonlight Drive" on the record player.

When you reach into a hat, sometimes a rabbit will appear.

The next day, her mother will drop a strawberry on the floor. When she bends down, she will find a chunk of glass under the kitchen counter, and she will turn it over and over in her hand.

Now, though, the mother closes the door and locks it. In the living room, she switches on a lamp. She is hungry. The little boy is running down the hall toward his room. The music goes on playing. Outside, it is dark. Ever so slowly the moon rises. Three black cats float down from the hayloft.

VENTILATION

The porch was cluttered, though at dusk under the burned-out bulb I couldn't have told you with what, and the screen door banged shut behind us as we walked inside. They didn't have central air, so the blinds were drawn all day, and in the evenings they opened the doors and windows to get the cross breeze, leaving the lights off as long as possible. The living room was a murky space, like a fish tank that hadn't been cleaned.

Dale was parked in the corner in his old mustard and brown plaid armchair, hooked up to an oxygen tank. This was the summer he was dying of emphysema. The TV seemed always to be on, even if he was dozing and Reba was in another room, washing the dishes or folding the laundry. As long as there wasn't a game on, she turned it down while we were there, and she brought out egg salad sandwiches and cold bottles of Coke and asked about the drive.

She was technically Evan's stepmother, but he'd never met her before, and he didn't know what was going to happen to her after Dale died. Reba had had to quit her job to take care of him. She was no longer young and had arthritis in her fingers, stiff joints. Sometimes Evan tried to ask her about the future, but somehow the words we had rehearsed in the car fell short, and he found that he couldn't finish the sentence.

Evan's father slept through most of our visits, so we nibbled at the sandwiches, looking down at our knees while Reba talked about him, how they'd met a few years earlier, how she'd gone out with a friend and seen him sitting at the bar and thought he was the best-looking man she'd ever seen. She'd never been so attracted to anyone in her life.

It was hard not to turn then toward Dale, who lay in the armchair in a pair of old sweatpants with his mouth hanging open and prongs in his nose. He'd lost fifty pounds at least, Evan said, but I'd never met Dale when he was younger and healthy, so I had to take Evan's word for it. I wasn't sure if Evan had either, really, but it didn't seem like the right time to dicker over details. He had spent a lot of his childhood sitting on the floor of his room, making up games while he waited fruitlessly for his father to come visit. I would have been angry, but he isn't one to hold a grudge. His mother had recently died, and in his grief he had turned even softer, like a piece of dough under my fingers. One night after too much to drink, he had looked up his father's number and unexpectedly gotten Reba.

On the television was a commercial for fast food, greasy hamburgers and paper boxes of French fries.

Reba took my arm and led me into the back bedroom. The closet doors were flung open, accordion-style, and she'd laid all of her dresses out on the bed. They were old-fashioned, polyester that had already pilled under the arms, nothing I could ever see myself wearing, but she held me and said that she knew we didn't know each other very well, but still, she'd come to think of me as a daughter. It was suffocating, being in that room, with its dark heavy drapes and the stale smell of cigarette smoke hovering in the air like a ghost.

On the dresser was a collection of crystal figurines and a large wooden jewelry box with its head thrown back. "Take anything you like," she said, gesturing at the dresses and the costume jewelry and everything, really, and I tried to stall, noticing all at once that there were empty spaces on the walls where she had already taken down the pictures. Through the open doorway I could see a cut crystal snowflake hanging from a pale thread in front of the bathroom window.

I thought it might be the last time we saw them, that maybe Reba knew something we didn't, but then Dale hung on through Labor Day and the end of that year. We lived two hours away, so our visits were short and infrequent, but we continued to make the drive. Dale got worse, then better, then worse again, until eventually he died during a heat wave the following summer, a little more than a year after I met him.

A few days later, we drove the same two hours south to attend the funeral. We'd been waiting for his death since the initial phone call and yet, when it happened, it still came as a surprise. It was mid-morning when we arrived in town, already a stifling, airless day. My black dress was stuck to my back in the heat. We stopped for iced coffees on the way to the church. Where was Dale now, I wondered.

Evan parked the car on a side street. We were early; the service wouldn't start for almost another hour. Nearby, we could hear the sounds of a game, of parents hollering and cheering for their children. Unexpectedly, Evan took my hand as we walked toward the field. He worked in construction, and his fingers were rough. As we drew closer I could hear a man yell, "Go, go, go!" and a loud cheer erupted as someone scored a goal.

We stood on the periphery, watching children in bright colors kick a ball back and forth on the field below, until a fire truck roared by with its lights and sirens and reminded us of where were.

We never saw Reba again. After the funeral, she sold the house and moved to South Carolina to live with her sister. Dale had been cremated, so there was no gravesite to tend. When we said goodbye in the church parking lot after the service and the potluck luncheon, she held me for too long; we couldn't seem to let go, and there was nothing I could say to smooth things over in the way I would have liked.

That night, in the dark, Evan came inside me, and sobbed, and for a second I thought that he was choking. It was just such a shock, sometimes, still to be alive.

THE SURROGATE WIFE

The woman went on a long journey to visit her sister. The sister was critically ill, in another country, and it was understood that the wife would not return for several months, maybe even a year.

In her absence, the husband hired a housekeeper. At first, the housekeeper only worked two days per week, and spent the night elsewhere. But they became more comfortable together, and the husband offered her a larger salary and her own bedroom and bathroom in the opposite wing of the house.

She moved in and shortly took over all of the housework, even tasks she had not done before and wasn't explicitly being paid to do, such as buying little treats at the specialty store and fixing the husband a drink after work. They soon became accustomed to this new arrangement.

The housekeeper quit her other jobs and, when she wasn't out shopping, spent all her time in the house. She became so comfortable that she began inviting friends over, at first just for coffee, and then later for brunch in the main dining room.

Occasionally, she and the husband slept together, but it always seemed like an accident. She brushed too close to him when she brought him a little glass dish of ice cream after dinner, or reached past him to loosen the tie holding back the curtains.

After eight long months, the wife returned unexpectedly. Her sister's health had dramatically improved. The wife let herself in with her key and was surprised to discover the housekeeper watching daytime television while she dreamily dusted the wife's porcelain bell collection.

Neither woman had been aware of the existence of the other. The housekeeper was nothing if not discreet; she didn't ask a question unless it was necessary for the completion of some task. Nonetheless, she had made some assumptions about a man living alone—namely, that his wife had disappeared or died—and it made sense to her that he wouldn't have taken the time to remove the artifacts of their life together. He'd never seemed troubled by his circumstances, and so she hadn't, either.

Now, though, the wife seemed more than alive as she stood in the hallway with her suitcase, slowly unwinding a silk scarf from her long, elegant neck, and slipping off a pair of chunky but stylish heels. (What kind of woman, in this day and age, wore heels on an airplane?) She appeared unruffled by the intrusion of a stranger in her living room. (A beautiful stranger, the housekeeper allowed herself.)

The wife introduced herself to the housekeeper, complimenting the state of the house, which was spotless and gleaming, and retired to her bedroom (*their* bedroom, the housekeeper now realized) to lie down.

A commercial for dog food was on the television, and the housekeeper snapped it off. The husband was still at work. A leg of lamb was thawing in the refrigerator.

What had changed? Very little. Or everything, depending on how you looked at it.

The housekeeper turned a decorative couch pillow two degrees to the left and returned to the kitchen to start dinner.

All afternoon, as she prepared to roast the meat, as she dressed the baking dish with garlic cloves and sprigs of rosemary, as she washed and prepared the potatoes, the housekeeper fretted. There, in the center of the home, were the kitchen and living and dining rooms, split between the wing containing the master bedroom (where the missus was, presumably, doing some fretting of her own) and the wing containing the housekeeper's room, which had been formerly (and, it would seem now, would most likely be restored in the near future to) the guest room, on the opposite end of the house, where the husband had lain in bed with her sometimes even overnight before the return of the heretofore unmentioned wife.

Well. Mentally, she scrolled through her contacts and former clients, wondering who might take her back when she found herself on the street with little more than a bag of clothing and a few weeks of severance pay.

In the end, though, she needn't have worried. The wife was standing at the front door with a drink when her husband came home, and if he was dismayed by her sudden presence, nothing in his reaction betrayed him.

The wife made a big fuss over the housekeeper's elaborate dinner, and insisted that she eat with them, going so far as to get up herself to set an extra place at the table. The wife had a skill for this sort of thing, it seemed.

She didn't seem threatened. In fact, quite the contrary: she began sending the husband and the housekeeper on little errands together. The grocery, the dry cleaner's. He had never done these things before her reappearance, but with the wife's blessing—encouragement, even—he didn't seem to think it odd to accompany the housekeeper from one place to another, when he was home and had the time, or to assist her with certain difficult tasks around the house.

It became apparent that the husband and wife had season tickets for the symphony and the theatre. He hadn't attended in her absence, but now they began going out every weekend.

He was happy, or unhappy. Neither woman could tell.

The wife had a migraine one weekend and bowed out of a concert. She lent the housekeeper a dress and pulled her hair up with an ornate metal clip. She applied nail polish skillfully to the housekeeper's roughened fingers. The housekeeper and the husband sat through the first two concertos but left at intermission.

That spring, all three of them packed for a long vacation. The wife had booked a series of transatlantic cruises, and the husband had arranged to work remotely. The housekeeper was indispensable, according to the wife, and she had arranged for a comfortable suite.

At the last minute, though, the wife found herself unable to travel. The reason wasn't really important. The husband and the housekeeper acted properly dismayed, despite the wife's reassurances. In all honesty, the housekeeper would rather have stayed behind, though she couldn't have said why; she had never left the country and felt far out of her depth.

The wife had arranged for a car to take them to the cruise port. She stood on the porch and waved as her husband and the housekeeper drove away. She didn't go back inside until the car had disappeared from view. Every few days, she opened the mailbox and found a glossy postcard from one or both of them, and she collected these in a pile on her desk until they returned.

One day, when they'd been gone for a couple of months, the wife noticed that the wooden shelves of her display cases were covered by a fine layer of dust. She couldn't remember the last time she had touched them.

Delicately, the wife lifted one of her porcelain bells. As the dust motes fell in slow motion through a shaft of sunlight, they glittered and shone, and she had never seen anything so beautiful.

CAUGHT

He found a woman on Tinder, but then she wanted to meet for the first time at her house. No woman had ever wanted to meet him at her house. They had some sort of rule book: a public place, a neutral location, an escape plan. Already, she wasn't following instructions. It gave him an uneasy feeling.

He parked on the street to avoid penning her in. There were two cars in the driveway, and he had no way of knowing which one belonged to her.

She had told him that her name was Audrey. It seemed plausible. In one of the photographs, a bandanna had held back her dark curls. She'd been outdoors, smiling, perched on an enormous rock in front of a deep gorge. She wasn't his usual type, but he was going through a dry spell. She looked earthy and efficient.

When she answered the door, though, she seemed like a different person. Shiftier. He wasn't sure, truth be told, if this was even the same woman. There was a slash of red lipstick across her mouth, but otherwise, she might have forgotten that she was expecting company, if that's what he was. Her hair was pulled up in a ponytail, and she was wearing a tank top and a pair of jean overalls.

So maybe she was the same woman after all, just brusque and unsmiling. It was possible that she hadn't remembered their arrangement—maybe that was all—or maybe she didn't like the look of him. He was attractive, especially in a shirt and tie, but still, everyone had their likes and dislikes, and it had happened before. He wasn't proud of that, of course, but she wouldn't have been the first woman to bow out before the night really got started.

But then that didn't seem to be the issue. She took his arm—a bit roughly, even—and said, "Don't leave the door hanging open," and pulled him inside.

There was a certain smell. He couldn't place it at first, or the sound: a kind of rustling. An unsettling sound. Then there it was again, the uneasy feeling, and he thought about how women compared notes and talked about red flags.

This Audrey person pulled him into the room with the birds. There were cages and cages of tiny multi-colored birds, and a few flying loose around the room, too, which must have been why she wanted the front door closed.

The smell in the house was faintly musky, unpleasant, but he covered his discomfort by saying, "This is quite a collection."

He was trying to maintain eye contact with her, to avoid looking back toward the door, but she wasn't looking at him. In fact, if anything, she seemed to be avoiding his gaze, and it occurred to him again that this odd, dowdy woman with her overalls and her room full of birds might find *him* undesirable.

Although he had lost interest the minute she opened the door, this thought perversely made him try harder.

"You have beautiful eyes," he said, but if she heard him, he couldn't tell. She was lifting a green parrot onto her shoulder. The bird squawked loudly, then imitated a fire alarm. "Run for your life!" the bird shouted.

He laughed uneasily and said, "Wow, he's very talented."

The Audrey person gave him a dead-eyed stare. "Yes," she said. "He can imitate anything."

He tried to turn on the charm. He smiled and said, "Maybe we could go sit down." There was still a bottle of wine in his hand; he'd already forgotten about it. When he held it up for inspection, the bird on her shoulder said, "Ooh la la," and imitated cries of pleasure.

Audrey seemed unfazed—she said nothing—but he felt his cheeks go red.

"It's a good year," he added, but now he thought that maybe she didn't even drink. He couldn't remember what they'd talked about before the meeting. He'd met a lot of women, and after a while, they all blurred into one, just another person who existed outside his body to give him sexual satisfaction. When he'd confided in his sister that he'd been meeting women on Tinder, she'd said, "Don't you feel like you're using them?" and he'd said, "Aren't they using me, too?" They'd shared an uncomfortable silence because she lived with her husband in the suburbs with two kids and a manicured lawn, and what did she know about desire? Nothing, he thought, observing along the hemline of her shirt a toddler-sized handprint made of spaghetti sauce, or possibly ketchup.

He'd had too much to drink and turned talkative, which he always ended up regretting. His sister was the oldest of the three of them and almost as judgmental as their mother had been before she'd had her stroke.

"Hey, asshole!" the bird screamed in his face. He was so startled he almost dropped the wine bottle.

"Careful," Audrey said, rescuing it, and she led him into another room, the kitchen, though it had apparently been outfitted in the 1940s and looked more like a set for a quirky children's television show than an actual functioning kitchen. The appliances were too large, the colors too bright. The cabinetry had all been painted a sunny yellow.

Audrey sat him at the red-topped table, in front of a pair of oversized amber salt and pepper shakers, and brought out two wine glasses. The bird had beady little eyes; when one blinked, the other continued to glare at him. The clock on the wall seemed frozen in place. He could hear the smaller birds scratching around in the next room.

"Would you like to kiss?" Audrey asked, and he couldn't think of anything he wanted less in that moment. Up close, Audrey's lips were chapped, and at her shoulder the bird's rheumy eyes were fixed on him. He imagined being pecked or scratched. But then she said, "If not, that's OK," with an insolent little shrug, as if it made no difference to her one way or the other, as if he were the problem, and he could imagine her describing him to her friends and laughing.

He said, "Of course," and he would have liked to have a slug of bourbon first but all he had was the wine still in its bottle on the table, and she hadn't even taken out a corkscrew yet and he couldn't very well say *yes, but it would help to be drunk first,* and she was already sizing him up, so he just stood, pinched his eyes closed, and leaned forward, aiming for her mouth. He landed an unsatisfying smack somewhere just to the side, and when he opened his eyes, she looked oddly pleased, as if she'd been vindicated, and he was sure all over again that she'd sized him up and expected nothing, or less than nothing—and so he took her in his arms and kissed her for real this time, pressing his body against hers. He was surprised to feel her give a little under him, and to feel himself react, but the bird must have tightened its grip on her because she yelped in pain and lifted it off her shoulder.

The bird hopped angrily across the kitchen floor, muttering and swearing. Audrey inspected her skin, which was bleeding now, though not profusely, and so she pulled him closer, fitting her body to his. He could feel her hot breath on his face and hear the birds rustling and squawking nearby.

"Maybe we should go somewhere more comfortable," he said, but he was still thinking of the wine; he needed something to take the edge off. He caught sight of the parrot, pacing back and forth under the table now, glowering at him like some evil spirit from a folk tale come to life, as Audrey ran her hand up one leg and unbuttoned his waistband.

He inhaled sharply, caught between shame and desire, and she pointed toward an open doorway. Through it, he could see a bed—also kaleidoscopic and cartoonishly oversized—and the blood pounded in his ears.

Then in the distance he heard a door open and close, and Audrey said, "That's my husband," and a muscular man carrying an old-fashioned metal lunch pail walked in, looking like a construction worker straight out of the comics page, and he knew then that this was their fetish—the naughty housewife, caught by her man. So maybe the husband was here to catch him and throw him out, or maybe to watch—whatever it was that got them going—and maybe his sister was right and he was too old for these games. He didn't know. But at any rate, he was here now, with his pants pulled down and Audrey's hand on his thigh, and the bird was still under the table screeching and glaring at him. The husband stood in the doorway with his bulging muscles and his lunch pail and there was nothing to do but laugh, was there, or cry, and close his eyes and raise his throat so that Audrey's husband could either cut it or kiss it.

THE PLAY

Carol and Adolfo were out walking when they saw the sandwich board blocking the sidewalk in front of a local theatre. The sign said ONE NIGHT ONLY, FREE ADMISSION, with an arrow pointing toward the theatre entrance.

Other couples were already making their way inside, and even though she had tied her hair up in a scarf and was wearing sweatpants and running shoes, Carol convinced Adolfo to follow.

They found two seats near the middle of the theatre. Almost as soon as they were settled, the lights dimmed and the curtain opened.

The set looked remarkably like a cross-section of their house, with the living room at center stage. It was flanked by the bedroom, on the left, and the kitchen on the right. The only thing missing was the bathroom. Carol had never thought about how small the house was, really.

An actress entered from the back door into the kitchen. The woman's coloring and build were similar to Carol's, though of course she was wearing a short white tennis dress and had her hair in a loose ponytail. She was quite a bit younger than Carol, too, and prettier. She left her shoes at the door, then opened the refrigerator and bent down toward the bottom shelf.

Adolfo was smiling, Carol saw, leaning back in his seat. Already she regretted her impulsive decision to come inside.

A man walked onto the stage from the other side, carrying a newspaper under his arm, and she saw with satisfaction that Adolfo no longer looked pleased.

The man was also younger, quite muscular, and significantly taller than Adolfo. Though Adolfo rarely brought it up, his height had always been a sore spot.

"Carol," the man called from the living room, and the woman in the tennis dress closed the refrigerator and walked toward him.

"Where have you been?" he asked.

She pursed her lips, pointedly gesturing toward the dress.

"Most people take a racket," he said. "Odd that yours is still in its case, in the hall closet."

"How would you know that, unless you were spying on me?"

"I wasn't spying on you. I was looking for my umbrella."

"It hasn't rained in weeks. Why in the world would you need an umbrella?"

"Stop making this about me."

In the audience, two rows in front of Carol and Adolfo, a woman took out a large cellophane bag filled with Swedish fish. She rooted around inside it, picking out just the right fish, then folded the bag up again and placed it back in her purse.

On stage, the couple continued arguing. The Carol character claimed that she had forgotten the racket and had to borrow one at the club. She stalked past the man and into the bedroom.

"That's what you said about lunch," the man said. "That you forgot it."

"What are talking about?" she snapped.

"Your wallet, the other day, or don't you remember?"

The young Carol tore off the tennis dress and threw it on the stage floor. (In the audience, Carol winced, thinking about having to bleach stains out of that pristine white fabric.)

They went on arguing for quite some time, the young actress pacing back and forth across the bedroom in only a bra and panties.

"You're so irresponsible," the man said, slamming the newspaper on the bedside table for emphasis.

"Oh, no," the young Carol said. "Mustn't be ir-responsible." She rolled her eyes.

"You're such a child."

"Mustn't be childish, either. Heaven knows, that wouldn't please A-dol-fo." (She sang out his name in a most unpleasant way, and this time, Adolfo was the one who winced.)

At his side, Carol was uncomfortably aware that they had had this argument in the not-too-distant past. They had been fully clothed, and the phrasing had been less dramatic, but she too had forgotten her keys, another time her bag, and Adolfo had accused her of subconsciously expecting him to take care of everything for her. Couldn't she just be forgetful, Carol had argued. Did it always have to mean something?

Adolfo had taken some college intro class and was still convinced, a million years later, that there were no accidents. Carol found this idea ludicrous.

When they were first dating, she had brought up a recent news item, saying, "So the driver intended to fall asleep and kill all those innocent people, I suppose," and they had argued so bitterly that she swore she would never speak to him again. Carol had forgotten until just this moment how angry she had been about it.

The actor Adolfo ordered the young Carol to get dressed. What he actually said was, "Stop walking around in your underwear. The neighbors will see," and she said, "Seriously? Are you *ordering* me to get dressed now?"

In his impatient sigh, Carol could hear something of her Adolfo. This made Carol both annoyed and, oddly, sympathetic.

"I didn't *order* you to do anything."

"That's good, because I'll do whatever I want."

The actress removed her bra, slowly, as if she were performing a striptease. "Do you like that?" she said flirtatiously, teasingly. "The curtains are open. Everyone can see."

Her breasts were larger than Carol had expected, with areolas the size of silver dollars. Adolfo, who had been shifting in his seat, was now perfectly still.

The actress crawled onto the bed.

The young Adolfo said, "Fine, if that's the way you want to be." Methodically, he stripped down to a pair of boxer shorts.

Carol began to worry that this was not a typical play, after all, but some type of live action pornography, but once the young Adolfo had removed his clothes, he merely went on haranguing the girl, who was by turns outraged and petulant. Even Adolfo lost interest in her magnificent breasts and began to fidget again.

At the intermission, Carol and Adolfo could barely look at each other. The play had lasted two hours already, and still, she had no idea what it was about.

"Would you like a drink?" Adolfo asked, and Carol nodded. He had barely returned when the usher herded everyone back into the house.

Inside, the crowd had thinned out, and Carol realized too late that she and Adolfo could have left, too. Now they were trapped for the second half of the play.

"Why is there so much nudity?" a man sitting behind them asked as the lights dimmed briefly and went back up, and his partner said, "They're showing their true selves."

"I agree that it's symbolic," someone else chimed in, "but I think it represents everything they've wasted in their lives—time, for example, and their youth and health."

The lights went down fully and silenced the speakers.

Ordinarily, Carol might have tapped Adolfo's hand, sharing a private smile in the dark, but instead she stared straight in front of her.

"You forgot my drink," the young Carol said, pouting, when the curtain opened. She was still lying on the bed in her panties.

Without thinking, Carol looked at the plastic cup in her hand. She had already finished the soda, and all that was left was ice.

"Not that drink," the young Carol said. "When we were at that club, in 1972. You offered to get me a rum and Coke, but you stopped to talk to another girl at the bar, and when you came back, you had forgotten my drink."

"Are you kidding me?" the young Adolfo said. "Now you want to dredge up something that happened more than forty years ago? You're unbelievable."

"Believe it."

The young Adolfo sighed again. He grabbed fistfuls of his hair and pretended to pull it out. "I've told you so many times, I knew that girl. She was dating my friend Tom. I was just being friendly."

"Well, you did seem friendly, that's for sure."

"Oh, Carol, let it go already."

It was exhausting to listen to them bicker back and forth, especially over such minor items. Adolfo had forgotten a drink once, yes, but what was the statute of limitations on such things? Had she really brought it up again and again? Carol could no longer remember. And the racket, the umbrella, what did it all mean? She knew that she had never played tennis, but there had been a time, many years ago now, when she had flirted with a golf instructor who was twice her age and married. She had flirted energetically, shamelessly, but nothing had come of it.

The bag of Swedish fish was dragged out again, and over the rattle of cellophane, in spite of herself, Carol strained to hear the dialogue, all those mundane bits of conversation. Adolfo was sniping about the laundry, now, and Carol suggested quite unkindly that if he didn't like the way she washed his drawers, he could get off his high horse and do it himself.

Quite unexpectedly, the young Adolfo walked to the forefront and delivered an interior monologue. He explored in some detail the early death of his mother, and the feeling that no woman would ever take care of him again.

The girl had a lengthy speech as well, the bulk of it about trying to please her father. He was an emergency surgeon who valued precision and control. She joined the young Adolfo at the front of the stage, with her breasts exposed, wearing only a pair of underpants, and talked about her father.

All her life, she felt he had never understood her. Had never seen her.

Carol squirmed with embarrassment. Her father had been a surgeon, but she had never talked to anyone about it, especially in such an obvious, self-pitying way.

She was successful in her own right, wasn't she? She didn't need anyone feeling sorry for her.

Adolfo glanced in her direction, and she looked at him and shrugged, shaking her head no. That wasn't her up there.

To her surprise, he took her hand.

On stage, the couple finished speaking and returned to the bedroom. The young Carol lay back down on the bed. "You're always telling me what to do," she said petulantly.

It was quite late by the time the play ended. Adolfo was holding Carol's hand again as they left the theatre. Most everyone else in the audience had given the actors a standing ovation, but they had remained in their seats, clapping without enthusiasm.

"Smythe is a genius," someone said as they left the theatre, and Carol heard a man say, "I agree. No other playwright can imbue dialogue with such depth."

"But what was the significance of the Swedish fish?" another man said. "It could have been any candy. I didn't understand why he chose that one."

A woman in a fur coat asked, "Why isn't anyone discussing the political subtext?"

There was a break in the traffic, and she and her companions crossed the street.

Carol felt glum, but Adolfo said, "Would you like to go to that pub for dinner?" and pointed toward a sign in the distance.

When they were much younger, when they could afford to splurge, they had gone out for wood-fired pizza and two tall glasses of beer. She had forgotten how much she looked forward to those nights.

The crowd was dissipating. Soon they were alone again, outside on the sidewalk. It was a relief to be standing there, just the two of them.

"Well, what do you think?" he said, and smiled.

THE COSTUME WEDDING

Jennifer flew all the way to Albuquerque with the dress in dry cleaner's plastic draped across her lap. Still, when she got to the hotel, she almost lost her nerve and went to the wedding in the black slacks she had worn on the plane.

She had slipped into the dress and then opened the bathroom door before unzipping her makeup case. "Don't you think it's too much?" she asked after a few minutes, leaning toward her own reflection and catching her boyfriend's eye in the bathroom mirror.

Barry sat on the edge of the bed in a pirate costume. He was eating macadamia nuts out of a glass jar and watching as she daubed rouge onto her cheeks with a big brush. He shook his head.

It was a flapper's dress from the 1920s: sleeveless, off-white, and pencil-thin, with intricate white beadwork and a thick satiny fringe at the hem. Her grandmother had produced it during Thanksgiving dinner, along with silk stockings and a bell-shaped hat sewn from off-white felt.

"Oh, I couldn't," Jennifer had protested. Now she dutifully pulled the cloche hat over her long dark hair, which fell past her shoulder blades and ruined the period look, but it couldn't be helped. Barry had found her a brown bobbed wig, but it was still on her bureau at home. Jennifer hadn't remembered it until they were in line at the airport terminal.

The hotel where Jennifer and Barry were staying was only a few blocks from her friend's house, and they decided to walk. Jennifer took small steps and held on to Barry's arm, feeling sweaty and conspicuous. She was a pediatrician, accustomed to wearing white coats and sensible shoes. The older doctors, the men, could get away with the occasional rumpled shirt, the tie imprinted with cartoon bunnies or kittens. But Jennifer was in her mid-thirties—the youngest physician and the only woman in the practice—and she wanted them to take her seriously.

The youngest and only, that is, until the previous fall. They had hired Dr. Whitaker fresh from her residency, and she had seemed solid enough until the weather warmed up and she started arriving for work wearing flip-flops and low-cut blouses under her white jacket. The other doctors were appalled. "What is the world coming to?" Dr. Drummond had muttered one evening after Dr. Whitaker had gone home. "It's unbelievable," Dr. March had said. "Do medical schools need to have classes on appropriate attire for the office, now?"

And Jennifer blushed, imagining Dr. Drummond and Dr. March seeing her on the sidewalk in Albuquerque, wearing this garish red lipstick and fringed flapper dress, with her big, bearded boyfriend dressed as a pirate.

It was a clear, sunny afternoon in late May. Someone had tied clusters of lavender flowers and white ribbon to the fence in front of Darcy's house. She had been Jennifer's roommate all through college, until Jennifer had graduated and gone to medical school.

Darcy had been living with Tom for almost six years, and Jennifer wanted to know why they had decided to get married now, all of a sudden. When Jennifer was eighteen, she had clipped her fingernails over the bathroom sink while Darcy shaved her legs in the tub. Now, though, they had grown apart, and Jennifer didn't feel like she could ask.

Jennifer had never been to a wedding at someone's home, and almost subconsciously, she had envisioned a movie set: an arbor in the back yard, or a living room wreathed in flowers. Darcy, she had thought, would still be with her bridesmaids in a bedroom upstairs, putting the final touches on her makeup.

Instead, white wooden chairs were lined up under a big tree in the front yard, and two women in matching black bodysuits and cat-ear headbands were handing out programs. Tom and Darcy, arm-in-arm, circulated among the guests, who were standing in small groups on the grass.

"They're Scarlett O'Hara and Rhett Butler," someone said. "Isn't that sweet?" But Jennifer felt certain then that the marriage wouldn't last. It was just too much bad luck for one couple to absorb.

Steeling herself, Jennifer had decided to approach Dr. Whitaker. The girl was oblivious, it seemed, and someone had to tell her.

Jennifer waited until the end of the day, when the patients had been sent home with their prescription slips and referrals. Dr. Whitaker was standing at the counter in front of the nurses' station, now deserted, looking through a stack of file folders.

She was standing there as Jennifer turned the corner: Dr. Whitaker, with her fair, freckled skin and beautiful cleavage framed by a clingy teal blouse, the faint trail of bones at the nape of her neck, her bright auburn hair drawn up into a knot. It was spring outside, but she herself looked like a fine, fresh day in the early fall, with the leaves turning colors and thin gold loops threaded through the soft tissue of her earlobes. "Yes?" Dr. Whitaker had said. She straightened, looking serenely at Jennifer.

"Dr. Whitaker," Jennifer said, and was immediately interrupted.

"Call me Sophie," Dr. Whitaker said, leaning forward and placing her hand on the sleeve of Jennifer's white coat. "Please. Everyone is so formal here."

Jennifer winced. "Yes," she said. "That's what I need to talk to you about."

Dr. Whitaker let go of Jennifer's arm and looked ruefully at the folder in her other hand. "Did one of the nurses say something? I'm staying late to get caught up."

"It's not that," Jennifer said, regretting the impulse to have this conversation. Couldn't she just have left well enough alone?

But what was the alternative? Watching Dr. Whitaker go on like this, day after day, with everyone talking about her behind her back?

"Your work isn't the problem. It's the . . ." At a loss for words, Jennifer zigzagged a finger across her own chest. "You know, shirts. Shoes." She looked down and saw that on today of all days, Dr. Whitaker had foregone the flip-flops and worn black pumps instead.

"Oh." Dr. Whitaker blushed, the hot pink creeping not just into her cheeks but also her neck and ears and pale freckled chest.

Jennifer felt sick. She'd had a small breakfast and worked through lunch. "I'm sorry," she said.

"That's okay!" Dr. Whitaker said. "I'm glad you told me." She clutched the file folder against her upper body and looked away, her smile faltering as she raised her free hand from the sterile white countertop and touched one shiny gold earring.

At home that night, Jennifer had poured herself a glass of white wine and turned on the stereo. Barry had called, wanting to come over, and Jennifer had told him she had a headache. Barry clicked his tongue sympathetically and offered bring her carryout Chinese and Tylenol. He offered to rub her temples.

Jennifer couldn't think of the right way to say no. It seemed too complicated to explain that she had a headache that couldn't be cured with good food or medicine or massage, that it wasn't so much a headache as an all-over ache, that she felt sick all over again every time she thought of Dr.

Whitaker's stricken expression, and that even though it was unseasonably warm for early May, she wanted to light a fire and lie on the couch in the dark, listening to sad music on her mother's old record player.

After the wedding ceremony, Darcy's new stepson dug a hole in the grass under the tree and buried a worn white rabbit's paw on a keychain. He was about ten, Jennifer guessed, and he gave her a sour look when he turned and saw her watching him. He hadn't worn a costume.

"Was that for luck?" she asked, trying to be friendly, but he turned and walked away.

Barry was getting a glass of punch at a card table in front of the house. He was in line behind Wonder Woman and a balding man in a cape. When Barry returned, he had pushed his pirate's eye patch up onto the top of his head. There was a pink stain on the ruffled white cuff of one of his sleeves.

"Are you sure you don't want any?" he asked, holding up the glass. "I'll share."

Wordlessly, Jennifer shook her head. Behind him, Scarlett O'Hara emerged from the house, smiling and carrying a wide white sheet cake. A few of her friends gathered on the opposite side of the yard, where they set up instruments and began playing dance music.

Barry finished his drink and joined other guests as they pushed the white wooden chairs back from the center of the yard. When a circle had been cleared, Scarlett and Rhett laughingly stepped into it, followed by several other couples.

Jennifer stood watching, turning the cloche hat over in her hands. "No way," she said when Barry bowed dramatically in front of her.

He removed his eye patch, took the cloche hat, and laid them on a chair.

"You're a flapper," he said. "They dance." He took her hand and pulled her into the center of the yard.

"Well, no self-respecting pirate would do this," Jennifer said.

But then she had a moment of doubt, and she didn't try to resist when Barry put his arms around her and pulled her close.

MY ONE AND ONLY

I hadn't seen Amy in five years when I found out about her death the way one does nowadays, through a posting on Facebook. We had been coworkers at a small tech startup, once upon a time. Sometimes a few of us had walked to a sushi bar down the street for lunch.

Over time, my relationship with Amy became awkward because she was religious and I was less so. No matter how many times I turned her down, she continued inviting me to attend church services with her. At first the attention was almost flattering. Quickly, though, I grew tired of fending off her advances.

Now she had been murdered by an ex-boyfriend. I was relieved to see that he was no one I had ever heard of. In the photo online she was smiling and looked much the way I remembered her, with a stylish haircut and a big shiny-white smile.

The ex had kept a copy of her key and let himself into her apartment while she was on a date with another man. He made himself a ham sandwich while he waited, and then he stabbed her 17 times when she got home, humming, after letting her date get to second base in the hallway. Or whatever had happened out there before she walked in the door. She was 35 and religious, so maybe not.

I sent a check for $50 to the local animal shelter mentioned in the obituary. She had volunteered there every weekend when we worked together.

The memorial service was a week later. My husband was at home with the kids, and I had two hours until my dentist appointment, so I stood in line to give my condolences to her mother. I'd never met her while Amy was still living. She wore a long-sleeved black dress with a cross on a gold chain. She looked like an older version of her daughter.

I never know what to say in these situations, and I stumbled through my lines. Because she was also religious, I thought she might say that now Amy was with Jesus, or take comfort in the idea, at least. But she was crying and seemed pretty grounded in the here and now.

Amy's mother grasped my hands, a little too hard, and twisted my wedding ring in between her fingers. "All she ever wanted was to get married and have a family," she said, "and now she'll never get the chance." Amy had a sister, and I knew that there were other grandchildren, but it didn't seem like the right thing to bring up. I also had two daughters, and it had become clear to me, if there had ever been any doubt, that children are not interchangeable.

Two years later, in early fall, Amy's ex-boyfriend went on trial. He had been offered a plea deal, but he had turned it down. In court, he pled not guilty. You almost had to admire the audacity. Police officers had found a wad of bloody clothing in a trash bag at the park near his house. When they tested the DNA, of course, it was Amy's. His was mixed in there, too, since he'd accidentally slashed one of his hands. Photos of the injuries were shown in court. There was more evidence, too, but how much more do you need?

He was found guilty and sentenced to life, no parole. Amy's sister spoke to reporters outside the courthouse and called the verdict a relief. She'd been videotaped every day walking down the sidewalk behind the D.A., both of them wearing sharp pantsuits, though the attorney carried a briefcase and file boxes and the sister characteristically had a purse in one hand and a Starbucks cup in the other. She could have done ads, she looked so polished.

The day of the verdict, though, she lost her composure. She was only able to manage a few words before she sagged against the podium and broke down in tears. It can help to focus on something. Now that the trial had ended, she realized all over again that Amy was never coming back.

Before turning away from the microphones, though, she dabbed her eyes. She leaned forward and said, "Thank you to everyone who supported us in this fight for justice."

My husband had started picking the kids up from the after-care at their school. Sometimes he stopped at a drive-thru and got a bag of burgers on the way.

Amy's sister looked into the camera without blinking. Our eyes met. I couldn't tell if she was talking to me. I had just gotten home from work and was sitting on the couch, barefoot, in a threadbare T-shirt, with a glass of bourbon on the coffee table next to the remote. Here I was, squandering my one and only life.

On the screen, she turned away from me and took the hand of someone waiting on the periphery. There were a million popping flashbulbs as she turned and turned and turned and walked away. Behind the podium was an empty wall.

I clicked off the television. In the dark screen, after a few seconds, I could see my own reflection, and I stared into it, waiting.

YEAR OF THE RAT

Danielle was scraping bits of food from her dinner plate into the trash. It was a tall metal can that she held open by depressing a foot pedal, but when she released it to walk away, the lid didn't close again.

The garbage was almost full, and a rat popped out of the crumpled napkins with a banana peel from breakfast draped over his head like a yellow wig. It was such a strange and funny sight that Danielle started to laugh. The rat looked at her with a scornful expression, though, and she broke off, embarrassed.

There was a temptation to put something poisonous inside the can and something heavy on the top, or to hold it closed with some kind of giant rubber band, but she didn't want him to suffocate in there with her old trash, and anyway, he looked strong, like he'd been working out. She imagined him lifting tiny rat-sized weights.

He shrugged off the banana peel, and the look he gave her this time leaned more toward inquisitiveness than derision, so she abandoned the idea of the giant rubber band (and the possible jailbreak) and let him live.

For the most part, they avoided each other. She left the apartment early, trying to catch the first bus of the morning. By the time she got home from work, her feet throbbed painfully and all she wanted to do was lie on the couch with a glass of wine and the TV remote. She paid little attention to the carrot peelings and shredded newspaper he left on the floor when he was finished with them.

The notes, though, she couldn't ignore—the scratches he left on the side of the garbage can or nicked into the wood of the lowest kitchen cabinets spelling out his demands. A bowl of ice cream, crackers. She never knew what he might request from one day to the next. Food, usually, but there were other items as well. A small blanket, for example, or a bed. She made one out of an empty tissue box.

He began to increase the pressure, waking her up in the night by scrabbling across the floor or leaping from one piece of furniture to another. He called her at work using fake names, pretending to be other people.

"Stop using the phone," she told him, but he wouldn't listen. He had been working out day and night, and eating her food. He was the size of her foot, perhaps, but stronger than she was, more muscular. In a physical fight, she was pretty sure, he could take her.

At work, her boss called her into his office. She seemed distracted, he said, and had missed an important meeting. Her work was suffering. A letter had been drafted for her personnel file.

At home, the rat scratched "your work is suffering" into the bathroom mirror. He meant this, she knew, in a more philosophical sense. He wanted her to quit her day job and focus on her true purpose in life. *But I don't want to suffer,* she thought.

"Tough shit," he wrote all over the linoleum, which she found scratched to bits when she got home the following day.

He was in the corner, under the kitchen table. The look on his face was pure disgust.

In the morning, she woke early and typed a letter of resignation. She fumbled around in the desk drawer for a pen, but the rat had stolen all of them for who knew what. There was a long list of items she'd had to replace, a hairbrush being the most recent. His whims were unpredictable. Somewhere, she suspected, he'd stashed away her hand mirror and a new box of paper clips and the Sudoku puzzle book her cousin had given her for Christmas, and someday she'd discover this stockpile.

For now, though, she left the letter, unsigned, in the drawer, and ran to catch the bus to work. She couldn't afford to be late again.

Instead she was late getting home, and she entered the apartment fearfully, knowing that the reprisal would be swift and merciless. The night before, the rat had requested a bowl of soup for tonight's dinner, but she'd forgotten what kind. She was exhausted. She had already left the office after quitting time, and she hadn't wanted to risk stopping at the store and coming home with the wrong thing. Her stomach twisted with a combination of hunger and fear.

But then, when she went inside, peering around the corners, he was nowhere to be found. She slipped off her shoes and sat down at the table. What to do, then, about dinner. She was still sitting, motionless, waiting for an idea to come to her, when she heard an odd noise from the bedroom. Soft scraping, then the click of nails down the hallway.

The rat staggered into her kitchen. He was bloated, disoriented, searching for water. Immediately, she remembered the black boxes her neighbor had baited with poison and set on the balcony. It had been a year earlier, after he found droppings when he went outside for his morning coffee.

She fetched the rat's tissue box bed and tried to help him into it. The rat kicked her hand away. He would have scratched insults into the floor, she knew, if he had had the strength. Still, she filled a shallow bowl with water and sat up with him for hours, waiting for the end.

ONE-NIGHT STAND

When he got up to go the bathroom, I looked through his nightstand. Tissues, a book on investing. ChapStick, a box of breath mints, and a long strip of foil-wrapped condoms. Not much to tell me who he was.

We'd met at a bar earlier that night. Both of us were drinking gin and tonics.

I fluffed my hair and arranged myself on the pillow, trying to look enticing. Maybe, when he returned, we'd have another go.

It was my first night off in over a week, but I couldn't face the thought of going home. All those empty hours.

IF THE ORCHID IN QUESTION WERE A PINK AND WHITE LADY'S SLIPPER

On the drive out to the cabin, Jeff and Miranda barely spoke. It was the first time she'd been to Minnesota. They had planned the trip during a happier time, when the suggestion of meeting his family had sounded like a promise.

The air conditioner in the rental car was barely working. Miranda stared out the window. An hour earlier, the view had been scenic: all those lakes and trees. Now everything looked the same. The blouse she had ironed so carefully was stuck to her back.

"How much longer?" Miranda asked.

Jeff shot her an irritated look. She was a modern dancer, and for the past two years she had been dragging him to Berkeley to the ballet.

They didn't speak again until they got to the top of the long driveway leading up to the cabin.

Back at home, her cat was alone in her apartment. Miranda had given a key to the neighbor across the hall, who was supposed to check on him once a day and make sure he had enough food and water.

About halfway through the plane ride, though, Miranda had become convinced that she'd given the neighbor the wrong key. Jeff had been leafing through the SkyMall catalog, and without looking up, he said, "Don't worry about it. I'm sure it's fine."

When we break up, Miranda thought, *I am always going to remember this moment*. She lifted the little white window shade and looked out at the sky and the clouds. She had always thought that she and Jeff were a good match, but now she couldn't stand a thing about him. She lowered the shade again.

"Could you please stop playing with that?" Jeff said.

Miranda ignored him. She leaned back and closed her eyes.

They were going to be in Minnesota for two weeks. Jeff had wanted to bring his son, but his ex-wife's parents were celebrating their thirtieth wedding anniversary that summer and they were taking the entire family on a cruise.

"Well, la-di-da," Miranda had said, but she kept her tone light. She'd been raised by a single mother and had never even been on a boat.

"Maybe next time," Jeff said, but she could tell that he was disappointed, too.

She was tired of being the kooky girlfriend in the baby-doll T-shirts and the batik-print wraparound skirts, tiptoeing around her apartment in her bare feet as she watered the plants. Jeff's son was almost thirteen now, and she'd begun to feel that her presence embarrassed him.

Jeff's ex-wife worked for a brokerage firm in San Francisco, and she was the type of woman who wouldn't walk around the corner to the dry cleaner's without running a comb through her hair and putting on a fresh coat of lipstick.

So Miranda had seen this trip as a chance to reinvent herself. Jeff hadn't even priced the plane tickets, and she was already planning to buy herself a cute pair of shorts and let Jeff teach them both how to fish. She wasn't squeamish, which she thought might score some points.

She lay in bed at night, happily imagining herself on the side of one of those 10,000 lakes she'd heard so much about, baiting a hook or gutting a fish. Someday, she thought, she'd iron his uniforms or pack his lunch, or whatever a person did when she was the stepmother of a boy who went to private school. Miranda didn't know. She didn't know, but she could learn.

Then Jeff's ex had mentioned the anniversary cruise and the whole thing had fallen apart.

On her birthday, Jeff brought her a box of imported chocolates and an orchid plant. They had been talking for a few months about moving in together, but then they never did. He leaned against her kitchen counter. Did she know that the orchid was the state flower of Minnesota?

Miranda couldn't have said why, but this made her angry. Of course she didn't know that.

"This orchid?" she said, pointing at the waxy stem. The flowers were ugly, she thought—like fat purple tongues.

"No, of course not," he said. "Only if it's a pink and white lady's slipper."

They fought. Jeff called and pushed back their dinner reservation, but Miranda was still acting cold to him when they arrived at the restaurant. She pushed up the collar of her jacket and didn't look at him. She wished she had just refused to go out.

At the table, she ordered a fragrant bowl of soup, and when she didn't wait long enough and burned her tongue, Jeff raised his eyebrows and said, "You're always so impatient." After the meal, when the waiter brought out a tiny plate and sang to her, she just looked at Jeff until he had to blow out the candle and take a bite of the cake himself so that the man could walk away from the table.

They had planned to go to a movie, but Jeff took her home early instead. After he left, she went across the hall to her neighbor's apartment and rang the doorbell. The next time Jeff came over, Miranda saw him looking around the kitchen for the missing orchid, but he didn't say a word about it.

A year earlier, on her birthday, he'd taken her to see *Swan Lake*, and he'd held her hand during the last two acts. She had loved it so much that they'd driven back the following weekend and seen it again. When the final curtain closed, he turned over her hand and kissed the inside of her wrist, and Miranda couldn't remember the last time she'd been so happy.

These two trips were the first they'd taken since her accident, and she was finally feeling better again. A little sore, still bruised, but walking on her own again. The night in Willow Glen, she'd been holding his arm, though he was the one who'd been drinking. They'd stopped for sushi and Sapporo; she often drank a sip of his beer, but that night, she'd stuck to water. She was already tired.

This was the neighborhood where they met, at a dinner with mutual friends, when they were both in their early twenties. They had flirted a little at dinner, but Jeff was involved in an on-again, off-again relationship that hadn't totally fizzled out yet, and Miranda had saved all her tips for two years to buy a plane ticket to Europe; she still had the idea that she might not get on the return flight. They both spent a few years after that fantasizing about the way Jeff leaned over and kissed her cheek as they said goodbye, his hand on her upper arm, where it might have led.

So now every time they passed the restaurant where they had first been introduced Miranda paused with a mixture of gratitude and nostalgia and regret, because who knew what would have happened if Jeff hadn't met his ex-wife and gotten married and divorced, if Miranda hadn't gone to Italy and met a forty-year-old expat who was also from California and decided that coincidence equaled destiny?

She stopped, but Jeff continued on without her, crossing the street, and she had to run to catch up, calling out, but it was crowded and loud and he couldn't hear her.

Miranda caught her ankle and fell in the crosswalk, unable at first to get up, thinking as the seconds ticked by that the light would turn green and the cars at her side would start driving.

"Are you all right?" someone asked, leaning toward her, and she managed to say yes. She dragged herself up and continued toward the other side of the street. The pain was so intense that with each step she was certain she couldn't take another, but she was terrified of collapsing in the street and being hit by a car.

She made it to the other side. There was a bench farther ahead, but she had to sit down on the sidewalk. She was fighting back waves of nausea. People walked around her. A stranger bent down and said something, but the pain was so strong that she couldn't answer; what she wanted to say was that she knew it would pass, if they would just give her a moment.

It was a dark blue flood, and she could hear music, loud music. Something classical. She felt so relaxed here under the water. When she opened her eyes again, though, she was lying on her back on the sidewalk, and she couldn't hear anything: her vision had narrowed in until all she could see was Jeff's face. He was frantic, calling and calling her name.

And before she regained her hearing, before she understood what had happened, before the ambulance and the hospital and the x-rays and bandages, her first thought was that everything would be all right because Jeff was there.

They reached the top of the driveway leading up to the cabin where Jeff's parents were staying. It was surrounded by pine trees. The lake was farther in the distance, out of sight, but Miranda knew that it wasn't more than a few hundred feet away.

He stopped the car and turned off the engine. He walked around to the passenger side of the car and opened her door.

The air outside was hot and humid. Jeff leaned toward her, but he was only swatting a mosquito that had landed on his leg.

He grimaced and wiped his hand exaggeratedly on his shirt.

Miranda laughed.

He said, "All right, pretty lady, let's go inside and see what happens."

GOOD GIRLS

Her name was Caroline. Or Catherine, or Caitlin—I can't remember now, but it began with a C, and for simplicity's sake I'll call her Cate. She lived in a little apartment with its own separate entrance behind her parents' house, though she was only seventeen, and was allowed to come and go as she pleased. My parents were more conventional, the brush-your-teeth-at-bedtime type, and I wasn't allowed to order Chinese food with a credit card they'd given me or call them by their first names. It goes without saying that she wasn't from there—she'd grown up in New York and didn't know the first thing about living in a small town where you couldn't walk down the street holding hands with a boy without some friend of your mother's calling to rat you out before you'd even gotten home. It was a completely different world.

Cate had two older sisters and a dog they'd brought all the way across the country in the cargo hold of the plane, but the only one I ever saw was the dog when we went into the main house to fill its water dish and let it into the back yard every day after school. The dog had terrible arthritis and could barely take two steps without a break in between, so we were never able to walk it in any traditional sense. Cate stood at the back window and said, my parents got him before I was born, and it was the first time that my faulty concept of a dog's life span butted up against reality. She got two apples from a drawer in the refrigerator and tossed one to me, shining hers on her shirt before taking a loud bite, and in that moment she seemed more like a character in a movie than a real person, at least any real person that I had ever known, and I gamely rubbed my apple against the hem of my shirt, too, because I wanted to be at least a peripheral character in whatever moody indie film this was. (I was a serious girl and even at the height of my powers doubted that I could hold up my end in a comedy.) Her parents were both at work, and except for the dog, the house sat empty all day. Perhaps this is why, even though she was only seventeen, Cate's parents had agreed to rent a house with a separate apartment and let her live in it by herself. Day after day, the house sat empty, and instead of skipping school as anyone else might have done, she attended her classes and went home in the afternoon, as she'd promised, to let the dog out.

I was a good girl, too, but I was absent from ballet because I'd had two chocolate chip cookies and a glass of milk the night before with my little brother and I knew that Madame Courroux would single me out in front of the class again; last time she'd pinched the flesh on the side of my lower back, under my ribs, and said, you have no control, it's disgusting, and when I looked at my thighs later that year in the hospital those words always came back to me but by then it was too late so I tried not to look at the faint white lines where the old scars had healed and I pulled my clothes back on as fast as I could.

There was a woman in the hospital who looked like a ghost—she wandered the halls, day and night, in a long white nightgown, and what we could see of her was long and pale and sickly; even her hair was beige, and maybe her eyes, too, but I was afraid of her and never got close enough to see. She carried a glass of water with her everywhere she went, and often stopped to take little sips, and I could never figure out what was wrong with her, except of course the same thing that was wrong with all of us—we'd lost our way, is all, as if life were an enormous forest and we needed to stay on the path. (*The* path, because, as everyone knows, there is only one.) What they failed to consider, or maybe never knew, is that when you wander alone in the forest for too long, you forget the existence of paths, or sun or wind or rain, or the sound of another human voice, or anything you might recognize or even love from your old life—and if you happened by chance to come across a path that led out into the sunlight, or if someone took you by the hand or carried you for days or weeks until you reached the path, you would no longer remember why you wanted to follow it or even how to move your feet in that direction.

For the first few months I was in the hospital, Cate wrote me letters, signing them C, with stories from school and black and white drawings around the margins. But I never answered and at the end of the school year, when her parents finished their sabbaticals and moved back to New York, she left her little apartment and went with them, and that fall she started at Columbia and the letters dwindled and then stopped altogether. I used to lie in bed at night sometimes and think of ways to respond, turning the words this way and that in my mind, but I was never able to make them cohere, and then the effort that it would have taken to rise up out of bed and take those first steps—a pen, some paper—and everything that would follow, you must understand, the writing, the envelope and somewhere a stamp, the journey to a mailbox, even to ask someone else to take that on—

No, it was an insurmountable task.

I tossed and turned, thinking of the dog in the back yard, feebly taking its steps. Cate kept her letters chatty. She didn't say that they'd had to put the dog down, because she wouldn't have wanted to say anything that would make me sad, but she didn't mention the dog on the return trip to the east coast or ever again, and I knew the score.

When I was well enough, the doctors sent me back to my childhood bedroom and I became an infant all over again. My parents watched me around the clock, feeding and ferrying me around as needed, and I didn't have my feet on a path, exactly, but I was at least on the perimeter. They took pity on me and didn't make me go back to high school again with the juniors—at the time it was the most humiliating thing I could imagine—so instead I got my GED and began waiting tables, like an alcoholic getting a job in a bar, but no one told me that it was a bad idea, or maybe they did and I didn't listen or hear, and I ended up back in the hospital after I passed out in the women's restroom at work. The most humiliating thing—repeating a year of high school with the younger kids—turned out to be merely a failure of imagination. When I woke up on the floor of the bathroom a handsome young medic was bending over me, though I had trouble seeing him properly because I'd hit my head and there was blood in my eyes and in my hair.

Outside the window, a cloud of sparrows alights, briefly, on the lilac bushes, and when I look down again at the desk the envelope is still there, unopened, with the handwriting that I would have known anywhere and the initials C.S. above a return address in Zurich. In a box somewhere I have all of the old letters, though I haven't read or even thought of them in years, and I have a different life now, and it's dizzying to think that lines scratched on paper 9,000 miles away can have this effect on me: I can't stop thinking of the apples, straight from the crisper, and the old, arthritic dog. Cate hasn't used the featherweight blue writing paper of our childhood—I used to send pages and pages of airmail to my pen pal in what was then called Holland—this letter is on a heavy cream stationary with several colored stamps. I slit open the envelope.

L, she writes, looping the letter in the old familiar way, I've often thought of you and been too afraid to write, or not known what to say,—
and I set the letter aside and turn back to the e-mail messages that are still in bold, unread, burning as they wait for their responses, and the document I must finish editing by tomorrow, and work diligently until my nephew calls from the other room that he has finished his movie and wants to go for a walk. My brother won't leave his office for at least another hour; I take care of their son twice a week, picking him up after school and sitting with him at the kitchen table

until he has finished a snack and the simple worksheets the teacher sends with him, so I turn away from the computer and get my shoes.

I was his age when my parents sold the house where we'd lived all my life and moved across town, and shortly after that my brother was born, so for as long as he wants me to, I'll hold my nephew's hand on the way to the park, or push him on the swings. Everything else may change and fall away but I am a piece of marble, immovable. He doesn't notice, though. He pats me on the wrist and calls me auntie, saying stay here, auntie, pointing at a bench, and runs off to climb the stairs on the other side of the play structure where I can't see if he falls or fifty other things happen that I could prevent if I were right there under him with my arms at the ready, but those aren't healthy thoughts, and I am all about healthy thoughts, so I stay on the bench where he placed me like a good marionette.

Cate wanted to visit me at the hospital, but I wasn't allowed to have visitors, at first, outside of my family, and when the restrictions were lifted, I never said. I was embarrassed. I didn't want her to see me that way. I asked them to take her a photograph of a door, something I'd found in a magazine in one of the art groups—it made me think of a fairy tale I'd read as a child, and I wanted to paraphrase the story for her, but I couldn't get that far. I didn't know how else to answer her letters. I took night classes at the community college for four years before I figured out what I wanted to do, and I met my husband at a bowling alley when I was forty-five, I've gotten a late start, I know, but when my nephew calls I am on my feet, ready to follow, and when he has gone home this evening I will read the rest of the letter and find a good pen in order to reply, or even study the time zones and find an appropriate time to call, and pick up the telephone and say yes, I can hear you, but I don't know what to feel when I think of it because I have pushed these thoughts out of my mind for so long, but the letters were one of the things that got me through, and sometimes, when we are lost in the darkness, the reminder that light still exists elsewhere is enough to make it possible to go on.

So I call. She has been living in Europe since 1997, her company is sending her to the United States for a conference, she would like to visit while she is nearby. It's been a lonely life, Cate says, sounding wistful, hastening to add that she enjoys it, for the most part, but has very little spare time. She is a scientist, always in the lab with her microscopes, and she speaks of it modestly, as if medical research were the simplest thing in the world.

I was surprised how happy I felt when I read and reread her letter, in that understated yet recognizable style, and it revived my affection for her, which had never disappeared but had been long dormant. Still, the night after we spoke on the phone, I lay next to my husband as he slept and saw myself as someone else might. There was a time (I thought) that she drew a knife blade across the tops of her thighs, touched it lightly to her wrists and neck. She is older now and no longer at war with her body. For a long time now, they have had a truce. There are many nights, now, when she will lie in bed and let her husband touch her all over.

I kissed his shoulder, but lightly, so as not to wake him, and he did not stir.

The day she was scheduled to arrive was a Tuesday, and I spent all morning cutting fruit and tidying up. At last, the doorbell rang. I rushed to answer. Her hair was cut in a short, flattering style, and despite her claim that she rarely left the laboratory, her skin was lightly sun-damaged, with a web of wrinkles around her eyes, but underneath she looked exactly the same, with the expression I remembered so well, and though we hadn't seen each other in thirty years, it was as if no time had passed, and we embraced, and I brought her inside the house.

We sit across from each other. On the table, a bowl of white chrysanthemums. We are the living embodiment of a poem by Ryōta.

In the afternoon, I serve her tea and petits fours, and when my husband arrives home after work I go to the door and say, come meet my friend, my old friend, who's flown all the way from Switzerland, and together we go to the table and I hold his arm and say look, here she is, here is Catherine.

WORLDS

It was a spring morning. The window was open, and the edge of the white eyelet curtains lifted in the breeze. Outside, a tree branch flaunted the green of new leaves.

I had drunk a bit too much the night before and could barely keep my eyes open. Still half-asleep, Meg lifted her arm and laid it across my stomach, pulling me closer to her body. That flash, only visible for a second: the pale white flesh on the underside of her arm.

She wore a white satin nightgown, exposing her bare freckled shoulders against the flush of her sheets. They were the faintest pink, patterned with pale rosebuds. The coverlet, too, was white eyelet.

Gently, I placed my hand on her head, and ran my fingers through her reddish-brown curls. I didn't know her well enough yet to know whether the color was natural. I hadn't met her parents or brother. But in the middle of the night, she'd lent me a toothbrush, and I'd watched her floss her teeth.

When she turned off the floor lamp, the only light in the living room was from the aquarium along the wall, and we stood for a long time in silence, illuminated by the blue light, looking at fish swimming back and forth.

She had built an entire world in there, with ornamental rocks and plants and driftwood formations that the fish could swim around and through, and when I kissed her, her eyes were shiny with the blue light from the aquarium, and the white satin nightgown was slippery under my fingers, and I ran them over her back and down, and in the morning, I woke with the eyelet curtains lifting in a spring breeze and Meg lying next to me, and I thought, yes, this'll do.

CHAPPAQUIDDICK

Her name was Rose Elizabeth, named for Rose Kennedy, a fellow Irish Catholic and the emblem, for her own mother, of what she should be: a hard worker, a humble person, and a dedicated mother with a happy, sprawling, close-knit family. It was the end of January, 1961. The previous weekend, Robert Frost had recited a poem at the inauguration, and the president and his brother Teddy had attended mass at the Holy Trinity Catholic Church in Washington, D.C.

There wasn't a time she could remember being called Rosie, the name on the back of her baby pictures. It had always been Rusty, or Russ. This was between the assassinations of Jack and Bobby, and before Chappaquiddick, when the air of tragedy turned darker, more sinister. Her mother—often drunk, then—couldn't manage the change to Elizabeth and instead called her Eelie, a word that sounded cold and slippery in her mouth.

There hadn't been any other children, and her mother had begun to feel that their family was cursed. She had tried to align herself with power and success and triumph, but it had all gone wrong for the Kennedys somehow, and that bad luck had been contagious. She turned on them, and also on Eelie and her father.

Eelie. Her mother said this less and less frequently. Then there was a blank space, and she became nothing.

When she was fifteen, she reinvented herself. She used her babysitting money to buy a two-piece and began to shave her legs, she got a friend to put lemon juice in her hair and let one of the Cartwright boys slip his hand into the waistband of her jeans, and she could feel herself sinking, and maybe her mother was right and she did have a bad gene.

It was a hot summer. Often, she snuck out of the house after her mother passed out in an old flowered armchair in front of the TV. One night, on her way back inside, she saw that her father was sitting in the dark waiting for her. He went to bed early because he woke early for work, but he must have gotten up for a drink of water or an antacid tablet and found her missing. It had only been a matter of time.

It was two o'clock in the morning, and here she was, stumbling in, ashamed—her lipstick smeared, the taste of Boone's Farm apple wine still in her mouth—and she didn't know if he could see what was happening to her, and what she would become. There was so much more that they didn't even know then. Through the gloom, she could see her mother, still slumped over in the flowered chair.

Later in her life, she could see that she was both the mother and the daughter in this story, as her mother had been. But when her father rose from the couch in his bathrobe and slippers, she wasn't thinking about that. The shifting light from the television illuminated his face and she could see him for what he was in that moment: a lighthouse on a distant shore, guiding her back.

Earlier that night, though, she had leaned back against a splintered wooden railing with a mouth against her neck and a hand inside her bra, her face burning with embarrass-ment and desire, and she had had the same feeling then that she had now. Let the railing break, let me fall back and be swallowed by the water, let me go under—and she had to close her eyes again because in all her life, it seemed, she could never decide whether what she wanted was to sink or to rise.

SMALL KINDNESS

Shelley finds him lying on a twin bed in the closet of their spare room. The room is full of junk—mostly boxes they've never unpacked under a layer of all the things she's thrown in every time someone was coming over and they were frantically tidying up. The bed is his, a spare from before they moved in together. The closet is barely big enough to hold it. There's no closet door, either—just a ruffled yellow curtain left behind by the previous owners. He's lying in there on this old mattress under a red and black plaid waterproof camping blanket from L.L.Bean. This is how much he wants to get away from her.

She yanks the curtain aside. "What the hell are you doing?" she snaps.

A year earlier, when she wanted to break up, he was the one who didn't want to call it quits. But now, now that they have a mortgage and a joint car payment and a fat little baby screaming his head off in the other room, now that they're really in the thick of things, all of a sudden, he's sleeping in a closet.

"What does it look like?" he snaps back. When she doesn't answer, he rolls over onto his side with his face toward the wall.

She can feel the heat in her cheeks and the back of her head. She wants to drag him out of bed by his hair and throw him through a window. She wants to stab him with tiny shards of window glass until blood spurts out of him in a thousand tiny blood geysers. Angry. She's so angry. But she's promised the couples counselor to *communicate*, so instead of watching him bleed out she pulls the curtain closed again and turns off the light in the spare room so that at least one of them can sleep. It's the best she can do at the moment.

The baby's standing in a playpen in the living room, hanging on to the side and wailing so hard that he sounds like he's getting a sore throat. Henry could come out of his closet bedroom and pick the kid up if he wanted to, but she's not holding her breath about that. The only one who looks more miserable than the baby is Henry's dog, who is also named Henry—the height of arrogance, to name his dog after himself, she thinks now, though she has to admit that when she met him, the sight of his little Jack Russell terrier made her swoon—and now they also have their son, Henry. Between the duplicate names and the sleep deprivation and the screaming, she's never felt more strongly that she might be losing her mind. They keep trying to change the dog's name, but nothing sticks. (Spot was Henry 1's not-so-original contribution.) Henry 3 is just "The Baby" or, when things are really bad, "The Monster."

"I wrote a thesis on eighteenth-century French literature," Shelley told her sister over the phone. "Do you remember that? Now I spend all my time hosing gunk off The Monster."

"Are you kidding?" her sister said. "I hope you're kidding." Shelley's sister has three of these things, and she walks around with a serene expression all the time as if she's

Mother Earth in her baggy maternity shirts with wet spots on the nipples.

"Are you a secret alcoholic?" Shelley asked. Her sister didn't answer. "Valium?" Shelley said. "Xanax? Prozac? Zoloft? Am I getting warm?"

"I'm hanging up," her sister said. "Joe thinks you're a bad influence."

This time, Shelley wasn't sure whether her sister was kidding, but she didn't ask—she was pretty sure that she didn't want to hear the answer. She just let her go. Saintliness aside, she doesn't have much to offer anyway. Their other sister breeds hairless cats and is even less maternal than Shelley is, so going to her for parenting advice is out of the question.

When it comes right down to it, their mother was a not-so-secret alcoholic, so none of them have much to go on.

Now Shelley wants to go in and calmly *communicate* that when Henry doesn't get the hell up and take care of his kid, it makes her feel *frustrated*, but she knows he would say the same thing he always says, which is "Jesus, Shelley, give it a rest," which is coincidentally what she wants to say to The Monster, but she knows he won't listen either, so what's the point? Instead she picks him up and dries his tears and takes him in the other room and rocks him for a while and sings that song he likes, and finally he settles down and goes to sleep on her shoulder.

In the morning, when they get to daycare, the person who meets them at the door is Miss Jessica—Miss Jessica of the shiny hair and the big smile. She's so young, still—barely out of high school. Young, not yet bitter and ruined by life. Shelley wants to warn her: Enjoy it now while you can.

Miss Jessica holds out her arms and the baby—always disloyal!—practically jumps into them. He doesn't even turn to look at Shelley as she leaves.

Still, she leaves. She drives to work. She answers her messages. She goes out for lunch. She's on her way back to the office when she finally sees Henry, walking down some steps, and it's as if the whole day has been building to this moment. Claire isn't with him, but he's coming out of Claire's apartment—a hundred years from now, when she doesn't even remember her own name, Shelley will remember exactly which apartment is Claire's—and even as she's feeling a shot of fear deep in her stomach, Shelley is also thinking, *Ah, so that's what this is.* At least things make sense now.

She drives back to work and sits at her desk, staring at her computer screen. Claire. Of course it's Claire.

He met her while Shelley was pregnant with Henry, and for a long time, Shelley was at the doctor's office with a full bladder waiting for an ultrasound or with her legs up in stirrups while the doctor checked her cervix thinking about how much pain she was in. Ha. She didn't know anything about pain.

Claire was young and pretty, and she laughed at Henry's stupid stories that Shelley had heard ten times a year for ten years. She put her hand on his arm and looked up at him with her big cow eyes, and he felt like he was sixteen again. Or something like that. Shelley had to fill in the blanks. For some reason, he didn't want to explain what he was doing with nude photos of Claire on his cell phone.

But whatever. It was bad timing—that was something they could all agree on. Shelley and Henry decided to try to make it work. Claire disappeared.

And now she's back again. Just like that.

One night, years later, Shelly has a dream:

She and a nurse are taking care of two babies in a hotel across the street from the hospital where she had Henry 3.

All night, she is holding one of the babies and talking to him. He's crying, but she is able to get him to settle down. "I don't understand why this keeps happening," she says after a while.

The baby says, "That's because you don't have much discernment."

The nurse has left the room on an errand, but when she returns, Shelley repeats the comment to the nurse, and says, "Wow! He's got quite the vocabulary."

The nurse smiles but doesn't seem as surprised as Shelley expected, saying only, "Yeah, he likes to watch the really highbrow TV."

They spend the rest of the night holding the babies, taking care of them, and early the next morning, before it's even light out, they take them back across the street.

As Shelley is walking out of the hospital, a very young man—young but big—tall, with broad shoulders and dark hair—is leaving with his parents. He gets behind Shelley and puts his hands on her bare arms, running his hands down her arms almost from her shoulders to her elbows. Then, with his index finger, he pokes her in the back, just under her left shoulder blade, and she screams and the spot in her back where he touched her cracks as she wakes up.

But back to Shelley and Henry and Claire. This should be the end of the story, but it isn't. Henry's apparently sure enough of Claire to sleep with her, but not to move in with her, and Shelley and Henry can't afford two places. Daycare costs an arm and a leg and they're barely making ends meet as it is.

So he goes on sleeping on his bachelor mattress in a closet under an L.L.Bean blanket for almost six months.

On his birthday, Shelley gets up early with the baby and doesn't kick Henry in the face to wake him up. Claire surprises him with an elaborate home-cooked meal she spent three days preparing, and tickets to a basketball game, courtside seats.

Suddenly, he feels ready to leave Shelley and move in with Claire.

Shelley tries to be a good sport, or be the bigger person, or whatever people are saying now, but when he finally leaves she calls all her friends and her sisters and says, "They deserve each other." It doesn't matter, though, she adds, because it won't last.

She's right, of course—Henry and Claire do split up—but it's three years later, after an expensive wedding and even more expensive divorce.

Still, the night he packs up the last of his books and compact discs and actually leaves, she's surprised by how spiteful she feels. She wants to be happy. They've been living in limbo for months. The end should be a relief, but it isn't.

Instead, it's a reminder of everything they've gone through up to this point. She's right back on the street outside Claire's apartment, her hands on the steering wheel, watching Henry bounce down the front steps of Claire's building. There were so many signs—all the things she didn't want to see, so she convinced herself that she was imagining them. She pulls over and watches him jog toward his car, flushed, beaming.

She goes back to work in a daze, and at the end of the day, she picks Henry 3 up from daycare. He cries and pouts as she dislodges him from Miss Jessica's arms. *Maybe it's genetic*, she thinks.

Henry doesn't come home that night. Or maybe he does, but he goes straight to his closet. Either way, Shelley takes the baby to bed with her. She lies on her side, crying, and the baby, who is sitting up next to her, reaches out his fat little hand and pats her hair.

He's never done this before, and for a moment, at least, the cloud lifts, and she thinks that maybe they will all find a way to go on.

Many years later, when the baby's long grown and they no longer have even cursory meetings to pass him back and forth, Shelley runs into Henry on the street and can no longer remember why they used to get so angry at each other. What went wrong? They loved each other so much, in the beginning.

They're different people now. They've both suffered; they've changed. Henry says hello, and they embrace, stiffly, like strangers. Shelley hardly knows what to say. This is a man she used to lie in bed with every night, and now she doesn't know a thing about him.

So they run into each other on the street. They say hello. They embrace and make polite inquiries, they nod and smile, and then they go their separate ways.

90 DEGREES, NO A.C.

On the news, there was talk of a heat wave. My fiancé and I were curled up on the couch. I put my arms around him and whispered huskily, "Why wait?"

He laughed and carried me up to the bedroom.

After a week, though, it was no joke.

We lived on the second and third floors of an old house in Seattle. The landlady had never put in air conditioning.

Most of the time, we didn't mind. In the summer, when I got home from work, I opened all the windows. Then I stood at the kitchen counter, listening to jazz and drinking a glass of Pinot Noir as I chopped vegetables for stir-fry.

But all that was in the distant past now. By the time I arrived home from work, my shirt was soaked through and stuck to my back.

When he got home that night, Tom tried not to make a face. "Sandwiches, again?"

I tried not to snap at him. "I made a salad," I said virtuously. But then I couldn't help myself. "You know, it's easier to make pancakes at 7 o'clock in the morning, when it's not ten thousand degrees."

Tom went to work later than I did, so he was responsible for breakfast. Dinner was up to me.

"It's hot then, too," he said.

We ate our sandwiches in silence. Then we took cold showers and went to bed early, with the fan on high and ice packs wrapped in towels on the backs of our necks. Still, we lay there, no covers, sweating, unable to sleep.

"Why is it so hot up here?" I moaned.

"Heat rises," my fiancé said helpfully.

The night before, there had been a faint breeze, at least, but now the curtains hung, limp and unmoving, at their posts.

We were supposed to be cake-tasting the next afternoon. The bakery was famous for its elaborate buttercream flowers cascading around and down the tiers of the wedding cakes. All my friends had gotten their cakes there. I had a brief fantasy about asking—no, begging—the baker to let me move into the walk-in refrigerator on a semi-permanent basis.

Instead of debating the merits of traditional vanilla versus almond sponge cake with layers of dulce de leche, though, I had to call and cancel the appointment because the hood of the car started smoking as I was getting off the freeway. The baker told me that we could reschedule in two months. I stuffed my sketch of cascading roses and hydrangeas in the glove box of the car and forgot about it.

This was a low point in our lives. I started staying late at work, volunteering for extra projects, just to stay comfortable for a few more hours.

Tom left work a little early and went to the movies and museums and the public pool.

I lingered in the frozen foods section of the grocery store, studying the ingredients of this or that brand of Rocky Road.

When we finally met at home, we should have been comrades in the bitter misery that had become our life, but we were both too cranky to commiserate. Weekends were the worst. It would have been better to leave the house, but neither one of us could muster the energy. Instead, we spent hours sitting on the couch watching TV in our underwear. My hair was at this time glued to the back of my neck by sweat. I don't like to tell you what I would have done for forced air.

Weeks passed. The temperature continued to climb. One oh nine, one ten. Our landlady stopped returning our calls.

"When are you going to send the invitations?" Tom asked. They were still in a box on the desk we used to pay bills and balance the checkbook.

At some point, I had decided to address the invitations individually using a set of calligraphy pens I'd purchased for this task. A page of my abortive attempts to write our names was wadded up in the little wire trash can next to the desk. I hadn't even decided whether I was taking Tom's last name or not, and his aunt had already sent us an engraved antique-style serving platter. The future thank you notes seemed like an impossible task.

We'd been together for the past five years. It seemed like we were already married, more or less.

When he said, "Want to fool around?" I didn't even need to answer. He could tell by my slow blink that it was too hot and sticky to bother.

I flew to Cincinnati for a conference and spent a heavenly weekend at a hotel with cold white sheets and an air conditioner set to seventy.

He stayed out late, drinking with friends. The amount of money he was spending on cabs started to add up.

We fought. When we were too hot to fight, we just sat near each other—not close enough to increase our body heat—and looked defeated. Glaring took too much energy.

Time rolled around. We didn't renew our lease.

He forfeited the deposit on the venue. I left my dress in storage at the bridal shop.

Eventually, I moved back in with my college roommate. She was still living in the little two-bedroom apartment where we'd taught ourselves to make cosmopolitans and watched episodes of *Sex and the City*.

My former fiancé moved back in with his parents. His mother started cooking him spaghetti and meatballs every night, just like old times.

At first it was fun, like an extended vacation. No more fighting over the remote. I had the bed all to myself.

But then the fever broke.

Tom called me, and we met for coffee. He'd bought a new jacket and cut his hair a little shorter. I'd forgotten how much I liked the sound of his laugh.

"We should get dinner sometime," he said, and I agreed.

I leaned across the table and smiled. I said, "Why wait?"

FEVER DREAMS

The bus was halfway to the campground, hours from home, when he began to feel ill. They were on their way to a corporate teambuilding retreat, where they would spend the weekend doing trust exercises and roasting marshmallows over a campfire, or whatever one did on such an excursion. Martin was in the middle of a divorce and hadn't read the materials that the company had sent out about the trip.

By the time they arrived, he had a high fever and the shakes. While his coworkers settled themselves in their communal bunk beds for the night, Martin was led to the infirmary—a name that charmingly connoted another time—and given pain relievers and a glass of water and put to bed.

This was his lot in life, it seemed—always to be ailing when it was least appropriate. In his early twenties, he had been invited to a bachelor party on a yacht, and he hadn't realized until the boat left the shore that he was prone to seasickness. He spent the night hanging miserably off the side of the boat, joined later by a pair of beautiful girls—girls he'd have been too shy to approach in his everyday life—and yet here they were with him, shoulder to shoulder, all three of them wretched and heaving. When the girls finished, they helped each other up and went back to the party.

In the night, Martin woke briefly as someone laid another blanket over him and replaced the cool cloth on his forehead. In his confusion, he thought that it was his wife, his soon-to-be-ex-wife, performing these ministrations, and in the darkness he whispered her name, but it was too late and the person was already gone.

There was an extra blanket folded up next to him. He half-woke again and again, and in this delirious state he mistook it for his dog, now long dead, asleep at the foot of the bed.

Three days later, he was well enough to ride home on the bus with everyone else, though no one wanted to sit next to him. There was an elaborate pantomime to that effect by the guy who always took the last bagel. He bent over backwards to get away from him, clawing the air, and Martin was forced to chuckle along—See? I can be a good sport. He allowed himself to be placed into quarantine.

He hadn't told anyone about his wife because he couldn't stand the thought of the awkward, pitying looks— everyone talking about him behind his back. He knew that they wouldn't have teased him like this if they had known.

So he sat by himself in his seat all the lonely hours back to the city to collect his car from the parking lot and drive back to the empty apartment.

Years later, at night, he would dream of this.

A HOT GIRL WITH A BAD ATTITUDE

It was the last night of the convention. Nearby, three young men dressed as the Tenth Doctor were having a conversation as another Tenth Doctor walked past.

She came striding down the hallway alongside the hotel ballroom, wearing tight jeans and holding a walkie-talkie. She was barking orders at a guy trotting along behind her. "I said to have them stay twelve feet back," she said, pointing at all of us. "Does this look like twelve feet?"

Everyone shrank a little. She was your mother, turning on you in a crowded shopping mall; the teacher leaning over your desk with a ruler and a cruel expression.

No mercy.

We were waiting in line—sitting on the floor, leaning against the walls. We were waiting where we had been told.

In the corridor appeared sinister little twin girls in the costumes of the Sisters of Plenitude: flowing white habits; white cornettes, starched and winglike, concealing the hair; their faces made up to look like cats. They marched toward us.

Blink, though. Where are you?

The twins walk past. Up close, under the nuns' habits, they are young girls again, accompanied by their mother. They preen and pose for photos.

The hot girl snaps at her assistant and storms off in the opposite direction. He struggles to keep up with her.

Your girlfriend emerges from the crowd, carrying two Starbucks cups. She's wearing a long, ornate Victorian gown and moving slowly. In ordinary life, she wears a lab coat and spends the day looking at slides under a microscope. What is real, then? What is fake?

Outside, it is dark already. The wind was so strong this morning, on the way to the hotel, that a woman's wig blew off as she walked down the sidewalk.

Your companion hands you a hot chocolate. The whipped cream is melting under the lid.

Slowly, the crowd starts to move toward the entrance to the ballroom. It is almost time for the performance. She takes your arm, and together you look for two open seats.

NOBODY WANTS YOUR HEIRLOOMS

After Shelby's parents lost the farm, they decided to sell everything they owned and move to Florida to stay with her older brother. He lived with his wife and two little kids in a waterfront condo with an extra bedroom and a screened-in pool.

Two days before her parents were supposed to head south, they rented a U-Haul and brought all of their furniture to Shelby's little house. Her boyfriend stood at the kitchen window watching her father open the back of the truck, hoist an end table, and carry it up the walkway toward the front door.

Her parents had sold a lot of things at their garage sale—some of Shelby's old toys, a few of her mother's cookbooks, other odds and ends—but they still had the good dishes and almost all of the furniture. Not to mention everything they couldn't take with them but didn't want to go to waste. Your half-full mustards, your toilet gels.

"Mother," Shelby said weakly, but she didn't know how to stop the train.

"We can't take more than we can fit in the car," her mother said, and there was no arguing with that, was there?

Shelby couldn't look at her boyfriend.

"Just kill me now," he'd said at the window as he watched her mother clamber down from the passenger side of the truck with a fringed lampshade in her hand.

Now her boyfriend was on the front lawn holding one end of an enormous bedframe while her father shouted directives. "We don't have room for that," Shelby said, but no one seemed to hear her.

After they left that night—her mother waving jauntily from the passenger-side window of the U-Haul—Shelby's boyfriend took the empty sandwich wrappers to the trash and swept the kitchen floor. There was barely any room to maneuver with her parents' dining set shoved in next to their table.

"Whatever you don't want, you can sell," her mother had said, in a tone that told Shelby two things. Her mother didn't understand why anyone would want so-called modern furniture when family treasures were available instead. And since they were so valuable, if one were inclined (for whatever reason!) to let go of them, finding a new home for said treasures would be a snap.

She had added, "We can split the profits 50/50."

Every weekend, Shelby's brother called to complain. They had both assumed that their parents—two of the hardest-working people they knew, the same people who had gotten up before dawn every day of their childhood—would get their own place as soon as they found jobs and got back on their feet.

Instead, they stayed at home every day, driving his wife up the wall. They had set up camp at the kitchen table. They liked to stay up until all hours of the night playing cards and drinking whiskey.

Shelby's brother went to work all day, but his wife was a stay-at-home mom. If the weather wasn't nice enough to go to the park, she had to keep the kids quiet while their grandparents slept past noon. The older boy had started making play cigars out of construction paper. The baby knew half the names of the characters on *Scandal*.

Standing in her own living room, surrounded by a sea of furniture from their childhood home, Shelby found it hard to sympathize. "Look," she said, "I'm having my own problems."

Her boyfriend had given her an ultimatum. He could accept the cabinets overflowing with her parents' wedding china, but he was tired of squeezing past one couch to get to another. It had been months already. Either the furniture went, or he did.

"Dammit, Shelby," her brother said. "You're so self-absorbed."

"That's not true," Shelby said, but then she couldn't think of any evidence to back up this claim.

When she didn't continue, her brother huffed and said he had to go.

She couldn't think of a way to transport all the furniture, so Shelby bought a Polaroid camera and carried an envelope of photos from one used/vintage/consignment shop to the next.

Most of the employees were polite but disinterested. They already had stores full of nondescript not-really-antique furniture that wasn't selling.

At the last store on her list, she took a deep breath before pushing through the door. The bell rang.

"Listen," she said, "I've got a house full of furniture and I'm not taking no for an answer."

She had picked up this lingo from her boyfriend, who liked to say it to his friends when he was offering to buy them a drink.

The man inside was on the phone, though, and hadn't heard her; once he hung up, she found that she couldn't summon the same bravado.

"Can I help you?" he asked, already sounding bored, and he seemed so sure that she was there to waste his time that she shoved the envelope of photos in her bag and asked what he had in the way of rings.

In an ideal world, the rings would have been junk and she could have slapped them back in his face and accused him of wasting *her* time and stormed out of the store, but of course she ended up liking one of the rings, and when she tried it on, it fit perfectly, and then she found herself out on the sidewalk with a $60 vintage ring on her finger and, waiting for her at home, a complete set of furniture that she couldn't get rid of if she tried.

Dammit, Shelby, she thought. Maybe she was self-absorbed after all.

She turned around and pushed back through the door. The bell rang. The man was scrolling through something on his cell phone; he looked up and raised his eyebrows at her.

"I have all this antique furniture, and I want you to take it."

"You do, do you?"

She took this as an invitation to dig out the envelope of photos and slap it down on the counter.

He glanced inside, then closed the flap again and pushed the envelope back across the counter toward Shelby. "No, thanks."

"These things are valuable!" she said. "You haven't even seen them."

"Look, lady—nobody wants your heirlooms."

Shelby blinked. At that moment, it seemed like the truest thing anyone had ever said in her entire life.

He tapped once on the envelope and shrugged. "Sorry."

Then he walked to the other side of the store, unlocked a door with a big sign saying EMPLOYEES ONLY, and disappeared.

Shelby wanted to take a tall white bud vase with a delicate pink rose painted on it and smash this guy's fancy glass cases. Instead, she went home and cried on her boyfriend's shoulder. She was trying to learn whatever lesson the universe wanted to teach her, really she was, but she just couldn't figure out what that lesson was.

She interpreted her boyfriend's silence as sympathy, but a few days later, he packed up and went to his mother's house.

"Oh, she'll love that," Shelby said, trying to be mean, but her boyfriend somehow took it as a compliment and said, "Yeah, I think she will," in a voice of boyish wonder, and Shelby ended up helping him carry the Xbox out to his car.

That weekend, Shelby's brother called from Florida. "Dad won't stop smoking," he said. "He's doing it outside, but everything stinks. His clothes reek. We can't do the laundry anymore. And I'm not even going into the toaster fires. It's ridiculous."

The wife was at the end of her rope. "She's threatening to take the kids and leave," Shelby's brother said. "I'm sending them back."

"Wait. Our parents?" Shelby said. Somehow she had missed an important turn in the conversation.

"You have more space," her brother said.

She turned and looked around the room. "Not anymore! I still have all their stuff!"

"If they leave here tomorrow, they should be there by Monday."

"They're going to be very upset about this," she said helplessly, but she knew it was no use.

Her boyfriend called late one night. (Her ex now, she supposed, but she wasn't used to thinking of him that way.) Shelby tried to answer the phone on the first ring, before her parents heard. They'd only been in her house for a week, but they had something to say about everything.

"Why are you whispering?" her boyfriend asked. "Do you have someone over?"

"It's not what you think," Shelby muttered.

They met at a park near the house.

"I had to sneak out," Shelby said.

Her boyfriend nodded glumly; he had snuck out, too. They'd had years of grief about living together, unmarried and childless, before the breakup. Now look what had happened.

"Why did you want to meet?" Shelby asked.

He shrugged. They ended up making out in the back seat of his car. The windows got so steamed over that when they heard a knock, they almost couldn't see the outline of a police officer on the other side. "Move it along," he said loudly.

His shadow receded from their view. The window was marbled by flashing red and blue lights. "It's just some high schoolers," they heard him call to someone else.

Shelby, in her bra, rested her face against her boyfriend's bare arm.

He dropped her off at the corner so that she could slink home unnoticed. The windows of the house were open, and from outside, she could hear her parents at the kitchen table. (Correction: *one* of the kitchen tables.)

Her parents were already half in the bag, she could tell. They were laughing raucously as the playing cards slapped against the table.

Before Shelby got out of the car, her boyfriend had said, "Do you think I might be able to see you again tomorrow?"

"I don't know," she had said doubtfully, thinking of all the hurdles that lay ahead. They had gone back in time somehow.

But her boyfriend was tired of waking up in his childhood bedroom and playing video games after work. He missed her.

"Maybe we could run away together," Shelby had said, only half joking.

Now, standing outside in the dark, she had one foot in the past and one in the present. She took out her house key and squared her shoulders before she unlocked the front door and walked inside. Her parents turned in unison, their faces as bright as sunflowers, and waved her over.

GOING IN TO PUT AWAY HIS LAUNDRY

The morning you find the wrapper from a pregnancy test in your teenage son's bedroom. Your heart beating fast. The thought that it might not be what it looks like. The basket cutting into your hip. The number of minutes until school gets out and you can ask him. The distance between this answer and that one.

THREE SHEETS

He shotgunned another beer before he called his sister. She'd been leaving him message after message; the tape on the answering machine was threadbare by this point. "It's about time," she said when she heard his voice, hers snappish as ever, because she was the younger sister and never tired of being disappointed by the scraps and hand-me-downs that life had thrown her way.

What did she want, though? She never said—at least, not until after the fact—preferring instead to play the martyr. He got up to find a book of matches and almost knocked over a floor lamp. Tiredness had made him clumsy.

Outside, it was starting to snow. He lit a cigarette, holding the phone between his cheek and shoulder as she rattled off her latest list of grievances. Then, "So what do you have to say about that?" It was a statement, not a real question, and he wasn't sure what to take from it. Sometimes he was in the mood for her guessing games, or at least a willing participant. Tonight, he couldn't muster the energy.

They went through the motions. Contrition (on his part, of course), and a short lecture—he needed to get his life together, tomorrow is a new day, et cetera, all the staples—and the call ended on a good note, he thought. He'd managed to hold up his end of the bargain.

She hung up the phone and said, "Well, he was three sheets to the wind." She drummed her fingers restlessly on the table. It was getting late. She stood and paced around the room, thinking, thinking. But what could be done? He lived two states away. Briefly, she paused at the window, pulling the curtains back and looking outside. Her pulse was racing. "You should have heard him," she said.

Her husband looked up from the newspaper and nodded. Her pronouncements didn't usually require much of a response. She just liked the running commentary to be acknowledged. She walked into another room. When he had finished the last few pages, he extinguished the fire and went up to bed. Downstairs, he could hear her clattering around in the kitchen, unloading and reloading the dishwasher, and talking to the dog. From this distance, he couldn't make out the words. The dog was old and deaf, though, and didn't seem to notice or mind.

Then he must have dozed off, because the next thing he knew, she was climbing into bed. He could smell the lotion she slathered onto her skin every night in the bathroom. There was a click, and a soft rush of air as the heat turned on. Next to him, she shifted and sighed and pushed her pillows this way and that.

He closed his eyes again and thought of her brother, and the dog downstairs in its bed, and his wife, and everyone else on this cold night, all of them turning and turning and turning, trying to find a comfortable position.

ON HOLIDAY

She fell in love with a man. They'd never met in person, but they had spent several months exchanging messages and phone calls and even, occasionally, talking face to face as they each sat in front of their respective computer screens. He had short, sandy blond hair and an easy laugh. He lived in Milwaukee and owned a small (one-man) business; she was a schoolteacher with no tenure and no remaining vacation days. Next summer, they agreed.

In late November, just before Thanksgiving, his mother called. The two women had never spoken. The man had gone into the hospital for something very routine, practically an outpatient procedure, and he had never woken up from the anesthesia.

The woman cried on the phone with his mother. She couldn't get away for the funeral, but she made a donation to the animal shelter named in the obituary and sent his mother a card.

Her parents lent her some money. She bought a plane ticket and flew to Milwaukee over the Christmas break. She rented a car at the airport and drove to his parents' house. They'd hired a service to empty and clean his apartment, and someone else was living in it now. The furniture had been donated, but everything else was in their basement, packed in boxes.

The mother had made the bed in the guest bedroom and left a set of clean towels in the bathroom. She let the woman see his childhood bedroom and go through the photo albums. He'd told her all the stories of his childhood—church on Sundays, sledding with his siblings, a minor accident requiring stitches—and here was the evidence to back up this Midwestern fairy tale. One of the boxes in the basement had photos she'd sent him, photos of her, and a book she'd sent on his birthday with a handwritten note in one of the margins. *Ask her*, he'd written, but the pencil had smudged and she couldn't read the rest.

She went to see his doctor, a youngish woman who also had short, sandy blond hair. (She was in a strange place, she hadn't been getting enough sleep, and in this state she wondered if it might be him, come back in another form, and she looked lovingly at the hands that could be his hands and the face that could be his face.) This wasn't the doctor who had performed the surgery, but the one who had made the referral. The doctor spoke to her gently. It was a tragedy, the doctor said. There wasn't anything they could have done.

The woman goes back to his parents' house. It's Christmas Eve. His sisters have come over with their families. The tree is draped in lights, and a fire is burning in the fireplace, and there are candles on the mantel. Everyone is drinking hot chocolate with little marshmallows. One of the children is begging to open a present, any present, or at least have a candy cane off the tree. Someone has brought a dog, and it keeps barking and running back and forth. It knocks an ornament off the tree—not one of the sturdy, Sunday school variety, but a delicate silver bauble that shatters on the floor—and a baby starts to cry.

His mother goes to the kitchen and gets the woman a mug of hot chocolate, and someone moves over to make room for her on the couch, but the conversation stalls, and soon the woman excuses herself and goes to the guest room. She's afraid that his family has grown tired of her, or they've become tiresome to her, or some combination of the two.

The morning of her flight, his father makes her pancakes with pats of butter and a generous swath of maple syrup. His parents walk her outside, and she kisses them goodbye. In the car, before she drives away, she looks back at them, still standing on the porch with their arms around each other, waving. Several times on the way to the rental place, she has to wipe her eyes.

She returns the car and boards the plane. The sunshade next to her seat has been pulled down, and she doesn't push it back up. There is a voice over the loudspeaker. She looks up, but no one is calling her name.

The flight takes off. An attendant pushes a cart down the aisle and offers everyone drinks. Someone jostles the back of her seat. All of the people on the plane are on their way to and from somewhere, and she is no different. She goes back to Colorado and resumes her teaching job and her life without him.

AWAY

He was sitting in a deck chair next to the hotel pool, fully dressed, reading a dog-eared paperback copy of *The Shining*. His left hand was bandaged up to the elbow, and he seemed unusually subdued, Mattie thought—or maybe it was just that she hadn't seen him in such a long time.

The wind ruffled the pages of his book. Mattie was on her way to the dining room, and she could probably have passed by without drawing attention to herself, but still, she hesitated.

In the pool, a pair of brothers began to splash each other. Jordan looked up, and when he saw her, Mattie smiled, practically charging toward him, the old trick of throwing everything she had into the hat.

Jordan got to his feet and gave her a hug, holding the book behind her back with his good hand. This close, she could see that he had a black eye—faint now, healing—but otherwise, his color was good.

One of the boys swam underwater and yanked his little brother down by the feet. There was a delay before the second boy bobbed back up to the surface, screaming and crying for their mother. "You get out right now," the woman said, shaking her finger at her older son.

"You on your way to breakfast?" Jordan asked, and Mattie nodded.

The older boy was hauling himself out of the deep end. "Look at him—he's not even hurt," he said, but the mother had already turned her back. The little one stuck out his tongue.

In the dining room, Mattie picked at her scrambled eggs.

"Where have you been?" Jordan said.

Mattie chewed slowly, buying herself some time. She and Tom had discussed this at home, at length, just in case. Still, she had to steel herself to say it.

"That's not something we can talk about."

He shot her a look of disgust. It was the same look he'd given her when they were children, when he'd crossed a divide—the thinnest neck of a river, the distance between his bedroom window and the tree outside—and there she was, hanging back, as always. Weak.

He shrugged and looked away.

For a minute, she wavered, wanting—as she always did—to give in. Tom had threatened her, though. If she couldn't keep Jordan away, he would have to take the girls and leave. He wasn't going through that again.

She fidgeted with her napkin, pretending to watch the news on one of the wide-screen televisions mounted on the wall behind Jordan's head.

No one else was scheduled to arrive until the following day. Mattie regretted lobbying Tom for extra time, two extra nights in the hotel, a full day to get settled, a little break to get her head together before going full-bore into all of this.

He was at home with the girls, whose summer school program hadn't started yet. They'd each taken time off work, used points to pay for the hotel. She could have been at the office right now, answering the message that lay like a coiled snake in her inbox, but instead she was pushing soggy scrambled eggs across her plate. No matter where she was, she wished she were somewhere else.

After breakfast, Mattie slunk back to her room. There was a message on the hotel phone from Tom. Their younger daughter had an ear infection. She'd been up half the night crying. He'd already taken her to the pediatrician and given her a dose of medicine. He just wanted Mattie to know.

Why? she wanted to ask. There was nothing she could do except feel guilty, but perhaps that had been the point. Often, she heard an accusatory note in his voice when he claimed none was there. *We ran out of milk.* A benign observation? A request, a complaint, a commentary on her lack of skill as a housekeeper? Her deficiencies as a woman? Her deficiencies as a person in general? It was a rabbit hole she preferred not to go down.

She didn't return his call. Instead, she drew the curtains and lay on her back on the bed. Her friend Anita Swanson had been encouraging her to meditate. Instead, she looked at the ceiling and felt sorry for herself. Here she was with a whole day, no obligations, and this was how she was spending it. Her friend Anita Samuelson had been encouraging her to think about herself. "What do you want?" she had asked. "Not Tom. Not the kids. Just you."

Mattie sat up. She wanted to get out of this room, this hotel, this frame of mind. Anita Swanson had given her a piece of Amazonite before the trip, to facilitate calm, and before she left the hotel, Mattie put the stone in her purse.

She took the rental car and drove through the little downtown with its striped awnings and flower boxes, its studied nod to the small towns of the past. The charm felt manufactured, and yet Mattie was inexplicably moved by it, nostalgic for a time she had never experienced firsthand. Maybe some window-shopping, she thought, as she looked for street parking. A magazine. A five-dollar cappuccino with milk foam in the shape of a heart.

Once she found a space, though, she had barely gone a block when she saw Jordan in the crosswalk heading toward her side of the street. He was walking carefully, she noticed, favoring one knee. She felt a headache coming on.

When Sheila had told her about this wedding, when she'd called Mattie over a year ago to say that her long-term boyfriend had finally, *finally*, proposed, she had paused, adding apologetically, "We can't invite Jordan, just you."

"I know," Mattie had said. "It's O.K."

"The ceremony would probably be all right, but my mother is afraid he'll ruin the reception."

Mattie was ashamed to remember, even now, that her first reaction was relief. She was grateful that her cousin and aunt had already made all the decisions, and she was off the hook.

Then Jordan and Mattie's mother got involved. She was by turns hurt, insulted, incensed. She threatened to boycott the wedding, dragging everyone into it, forcing them to choose sides. The two sisters had fought bitterly.

Finally, to keep the peace, Mattie's cousin and aunt had given in and sent an invitation to Jordan. (At his last known address, no plus-one, Sheila told Mattie over the phone.) Their mothers had barely spoken in months.

Last Mattie had heard, though, Jordan hadn't even returned the RSVP card. Now here he was.

As he crossed onto the sidewalk in front of her, Jordan abruptly clutched his chest and dropped to one knee.

Mattie screamed a little and ran toward him, holding her purse strap in one hand, frantically looking around for someone who could help, but there was no one there. He was so far away, and she had put on low heels and a skirt for a day of sightseeing—why couldn't she have worn sneakers?—but when she reached Jordan, she could see that he was fumbling on the ground for a book of matches. In his breast pocket was a pack of cigarettes, still his old brand.

"Jordan," Mattie said, and she reached down to help him up, but he wouldn't stand at first. He was patting the ground with his unbandaged hand, not quite able to get a handle on the matchbook, so Mattie picked it up for him, then hoisted him up with some difficulty.

"I thought you weren't drinking," Mattie said.

"I'm not," Jordan said. "I'm didn't."

Dryly, Mattie said, "You'm didn't? Really?" She sighed, turning them both around toward the rental car.

She drove slowly, but the speed bumps in the hotel parking lot did him in. She was pulling into a parking space when he began to dry heave, eyes closed, his head pressed back against the headrest. Mattie ran around to the passenger side, yanking the door open and pulling him out of the car and into the bushes.

As she waited, she thought, *At least I won't have to pay the fee to clean the car*, and chewed her nails. When he was finished, she wiped his mouth with a tissue and helped him up to his room.

Mattie had come to the wedding alone because Tom didn't want to bring the girls. Sheila was already seven months pregnant, and he thought it was setting a bad example for them.

They were too young to remember, or perhaps even to notice, Mattie argued, but Tom said they would notice all right—what they were too young for was making sense of it. What they understood, at the moment, was that grown adults got married, and then they could have babies. He wanted them to know that marriage was important, and that it was a first step, not something that came later or not at all. Tom was very big on rules and order.

Never mind, she told him in the end. So I'll have some time to myself. It'll be relaxing.

Jordan woke up in a daze. Mattie's cell phone was ringing. "Yes," she said as she picked up, trying to whisper. She'd spent most of the afternoon sitting cross-legged on the end of Jordan's bed, watching television with the sound turned down and the captions on.

"I'm not here," Jordan mumbled. "Tell them I'm not here."

"Who is that?" Tom asked.

Reluctantly, Mattie said, "You know."

Tom swore softly. "I thought he wasn't going to be there," he said, through such a clear connection that Mattie felt sure Jordan could hear him, and she winced a little. "Don't get caught up in that again," Tom said.

When she didn't answer, he said, "Mattie. You promised."

"I know," she said. "I'm not."

"This is so frustrating," he said.

"I have to go."

She didn't have to see Tom to know that he was frowning. He would be sitting at the big desk in his home office, leaning forward. He would have picked up his stress ball by now, the one that looked like a miniature football, and would be squeezing it in his free hand.

"Do not forget what we talked about," he said. "I'm serious this time."

"I'm not forgetting," Mattie said quietly, and then she repeated it a second time, louder, to make sure that he heard her.

Mattie went downstairs and brought back a salad for herself and a container of chicken soup for Jordan. She set them on the little table by the window. "Do you feel well enough to eat something?" she asked.

He didn't respond. She couldn't tell whether he was still dozing or just lying with his eyes closed. Mattie pushed the curtains aside and looked down at the pool. It was still light out, and a few kids were frolicking around in the water. Several teenagers sat along the edge with their feet in the pool. An older man with a beer was ogling a girl in a bikini who kept throwing her head back and laughing. Mattie wished she had a glass of wine, a shot, anything—but of course drinking was out of the question.

She dropped the curtain and pulled out one of the chairs. She sat down at the table. She pushed a plastic fork through the clear poly wrapping and popped open her salad. At home, Tom would have made veal piccata or grilled baby lamb chops. Someone would be setting the table. Mattie hadn't even asked about their younger daughter, the one with the ear infection. Poor baby. Mattie shook her head. Tom would have said something if things had gotten worse. She picked through the salad for a cherry tomato.

She woke up Friday morning with the waistband of her skirt twisted halfway around and the fabric bunched up under one side. Even though she'd gotten the extra sheet and blanket out of the closet and rolled herself up in them, she was still cold. She was lying on top of the quilt, toward the foot of the bed.

It took her a few seconds to identify the scratching noise that had woken her. The curtains were still drawn, and she couldn't tell what time of day it was. In the dim light of the room, she could see Jordan rifling through her purse.

"What're you doing?" she asked hoarsely.

His head jerked up.

"I'm just looking for a mint," he said.

He always could lie right to her face.

"There might be a tin of Altoids," she said curtly. "Keep looking."

Jordan gave up the pretense. "Could I borrow twenty dollars?"

"I didn't bring any cash."

Mattie rolled over and closed her eyes again. Before she'd gone to sleep, she'd stuffed her driver's license and a small wad of bills and credit cards inside her bra.

The scratching noise continued. "You must've brought something," he muttered.

She heard her wallet snap open. He leafed through a handful of baby pictures of her daughters, her library card, and an expired Red Cross CPR certification. "Come on," he said. "How are you paying for this trip?"

Mattie pretended to be asleep.

"Mattie, please," he coaxed. "I haven't eaten since yesterday. Just lend me twenty dollars. I'm good for it." When she didn't answer, he said, "Fifteen? Ten? Even ten would be something. Mattie."

Silence.

Jordan sighed. "You've got to have some cash. A card, at least. You're paying for a room."

She could feel him staring at her.

"This is stupid." With his good hand, he tossed the wallet down and dumped the contents of her purse on the table. "You're on vacation. You must have money somewhere."

Reluctantly, she turned over to face him. "Tom prepaid for the room."

"Oh, Tom." Jordan rolled his eyes. "And where is your puppeteer, anyway?"

"Stop it."

He scoffed. "You're such a baby." He crossed the room and stood over her, looking down. Mattie didn't flinch.

"What about spending money? There's no way to pre-pay for everything."

"I don't have any money, Jordan."

"Liar."

For a minute, Mattie held her breath, afraid that he would lift her off the bed and shake her until the money fell out.

He leaned down. She could feel his breath on her cheek.

"Someone should drive you into the desert and leave you for the vultures to eat," he said.

Mattie heard the door open and close.

She lay on the bed until she was sure he was gone. Then she got up, stiff and exhausted, to retrieve the contents of her purse and limp out to the bank of elevators.

Back inside her room, she locked the deadbolt and the chain and turned off her cell phone. She took a hot shower and put on pajamas and, at last, fell into a fitful sleep.

Mattie was late to the rehearsal. Though she wasn't part of the wedding party, Sheila had invited her to watch. She eased open the door of the hall and tiptoed in.

Her mother, sitting in the back row, caught her hand. Mattie leaned down and hugged her from the side, careful not to spill her coffee. She'd been up for nearly an hour and still felt groggy.

She would have preferred to sit elsewhere, but her mother stage-whispered to the entire row to move down one so that Mattie could sit next to her, setting off a domino effect of elderly relatives whispering down the line and then gathering their sweaters and bags and rustling from one seat to the next.

Apologetically, Mattie mouthed, "Thank you," to everyone in the row. All of the bridesmaids had turned to look at them and her cheeks were hot.

In a front corner of the room, someone began banging out Pachelbel's Canon in D on the piano.

Her mother patted her hand and whispered, "Have you seen Jordan?"

Mattie shook her head.

She dug through her purse, pretending to look for a travel pack of tissues, a tube of ChapStick, anything. That was when she realized that the stone Anita Swanson had given her, the little piece of Amazonite, was gone. It must have fallen out in Jordan's room, and she hadn't seen it when she'd picked up the other items. Maybe it had rolled under the table or landed along the wall under the air conditioning unit.

All Mattie had left now were the questions from the other Anita. Her voice had been low and serious when she'd asked, "What do *you* want?"

Mattie sipped the coffee slowly and wished she had taken a couple of Tylenol before she'd left her hotel room.

The bottle was on the bathroom counter next to her makeup case.

As they were leaving the hall, her mother grasped her arm. A man was being arrested across the street, and of course Mattie knew exactly what her mother was thinking, because she'd had the same thought. It wasn't Jordan, though—just another dark-haired man in handcuffs.

The morning of the wedding, on her way to breakfast, Mattie saw the two boys in the pool again. Their mother was lying in the sun where she had been the first time Mattie had seen her, and Mattie turned nervously toward the deck chair on the other side, half-expecting to see Jordan sitting there with his bandaged hand and his book. The chair was empty.

The older boy swam underwater and yanked his little brother down by the feet. This time there was a long delay. The water closed over the younger boy's head so completely that both brothers disappeared from Mattie's view.

Absentmindedly, the mother scratched her arm. Her eyes were closed, and she appeared not to notice that the noise from the pool had ceased.

The boys resurfaced at almost the same time, both thrashing and screaming and crying. The younger one had managed to kick the older boy hard in the face.

"Mom!" he shrieked. "Did you hear me?"

Languorously, without opening her eyes, the woman said, "You got what you deserved then, didn't you?"

"You'll pay for this," the older boy hissed at his younger brother, pressing his hand against his hurt cheek, and they both went on crying noisily, hoping, Mattie thought, to elicit some sympathy.

Finally, the wedding.

All around the room, there were children: boys in tiny suits and ties, girls in pastel dresses. Abruptly, Mattie thought that Tom might have changed his mind and brought their daughters after all. She craned her neck, looking around the entire room, but they weren't there.

Still, long after she knew that she wouldn't catch sight of them, she kept looking—the way, at home, she would repeatedly open the same cupboard looking for something better. A better drink, a better snack. No matter how many times she opened the door, though, the items inside were always the same.

This was just as fruitless, and she didn't know why she couldn't stop herself. Of course he wasn't there. He had said he wouldn't come, so he didn't.

Tom was a different type of person. His family was cufflinks and 401(k)s. Always had been, always would be. Even after eleven years, he didn't understand her.

The pianist was playing softly as everyone in the room bustled around, getting settled. Mattie was aware of a buzz of nervous energy in the room, the feverishness she remembered from when she was younger, backstage before a play.

Her mother caught her attention, waving and gesturing toward the empty seat next to her. The space between the rows of seats was too narrow, and Mattie apologized as she stepped over other people's feet to get to the chair. Nearby, someone was wearing too much aftershave.

It felt oddly like any other wedding. At the first notes of the Pachelbel, a hush fell over the crowd. The bridesmaids marched down the aisle unnaturally slowly, trying to match their gait to the piano music. The flower girl tossed each handful of pink petals from her basket as if the performance were going to get her into college.

Sheila emerged from the back of the room, her arm looped through her father's. She was as big as a house, in a form-fitting white satin dress, and she was absolutely radiant. Everyone was crying—Sheila's father, the groom, even Mattie herself—watching her cousin walk down the aisle, Mattie couldn't stop sniffling and dabbing her eyes.

It was the expression on the groom's face as he looked at Sheila that did Mattie in. She could remember her own wedding, when Tom looked at her the same way, before eleven years of apathy settled over them.

Sheila arrived at the end of the aisle, and her father handed her over. It was the last week Sheila's doctor was willing to let her travel before the baby was born.

Jordan cornered Mattie at the reception. He was wearing a dark gray suit, and Mattie noticed several of the bridesmaids watching him. His bandaged hand was almost completely concealed by the sleeve of his jacket, and he'd showered and combed his hair. The bones of his face were a little too prominent, but he was still a handsome man, with broad shoulders and big brown eyes. He hadn't completely ruined his looks.

Mattie was sitting with their grandmother, who said, "You must be so happy for an excuse to see each other," and before Mattie could think of a reply, Jordan said, "Not this girl," jerking his thumb toward Mattie. "She's been avoiding me all weekend."

"I can't believe that," their grandmother said, and Mattie laughed weakly.

"Do you have a few bucks I could borrow?" Jordan asked, eyeing Mattie's purse.

Their grandmother said, "Oh, is it a cash bar? I might have a few dollars." She began rummaging through her bag.

Jordan pulled over an empty chair and sat down too close to Mattie. "Let's run next door to the ATM. You can get some out there."

"I don't have any way to do that," Mattie said.

"There's got to be a way."

"No. Stop it."

He sneered at her. "Fine. I'll just ask Mom for the money."

Triumphantly, their grandmother pulled three rumpled one-dollar bills out of her purse and gave them to Jordan. "You go get yourself a glass of champagne," she said.

"Thank you," Jordan said, not virtuous enough to refuse her grocery money, and Mattie wished he would just die already and set them all free. He got up and left without saying goodbye, and the D.J. was playing an old Carly Simon song, "Coming Around Again," and Mattie felt so guilty that she couldn't help crying again.

Her grandmother patted her hand. "Weddings make everyone emotional," she said, and Mattie felt a wave of despair, thick and viscous.

Across the room, her grandfather was holding his arms out, dancing in a slow circle with the little flower girl.

As if she could hear Mattie's thoughts, her grandmother said, "There were times I thought we weren't going to make it."

Her grandparents had been married more than sixty years, since she was eighteen and he was nineteen. Mattie said, "How did you?"

"I don't know," she said. She squeezed Mattie's hand. "Just hang in there."

Mattie had an early flight the next morning. She was awake before the alarm went off, ready to shower and dress, ready to drag her suitcase downstairs, ready to check out of the hotel and slough off everything around her. She had already gotten off the elevator and was partway down the hall when she realized that she'd gotten off on the wrong floor. Jordan's room was only two doors down.

She walked back to the bank of elevators and pushed the button. While she was waiting, the door to his room opened. One of the bridesmaids from the night before crept out on tiptoe, holding a pair of slingback pumps by the straps, and closed the door soundlessly behind her. Her dress and hair were crumpled, and there was a long run in one of her ny-lons.

When the bridesmaid looked up and saw Mattie, she smiled, looking chagrined, and said, "Late night."

Mattie nodded and smiled noncommittally, playing the role of anonymous hotel guest, passing no judgment, and the girl crept down the hall toward her own room.

Watching her, Mattie wondered if the bridesmaid had also held his head and spent half the night cleaning the bathroom.

On the way to the car rental return, Mattie followed a woman who'd filled the entire back window of her car with tiny stuffed animals. How did she keep them in place? For that matter, how could she see to drive? Maybe she had left strategically empty areas that so that she could at least use her mirrors to see behind her. If so, they were invisible to Mattie.

All of this seemed somehow like a metaphor, but what did it mean? Was she supposed to notice the obstruction, or the as-yet-unseen pathways out of chaos? Mattie wondered what the two Anitas would make of it.

I heard about your cousin's wedding, the message had said. Mattie had been sitting at her computer at work as she read it. *I'm supposed to fly down there for meetings on Thursday and Friday afternoon, and I decided to stay through the weekend. I'll be at the Marriott downtown. Let me know if you'd like to get together.*

Then, breaking an unspoken rule, he had added, *I still think about you all the time.*

Mattie took a cab home from the airport. From the curb in front of the house, as soon as she opened the door, before she'd even handed the driver the bills or taken out her suitcase, she could hear the girls in the back yard, squealing with laughter.

She walked through the house to the sliding glass door, leaving her suitcase by the front staircase so that she could take it up to the bedroom when she came back inside.

The girls were on the back lawn playing with a brown puppy so little and fluffy that he looked like a stuffed animal. Tom had always said no to a dog, no matter how their daughters had begged, and Mattie looked at him, sitting on a chair on the porch in his shirtsleeves.

"He's not ours!" Tom said quickly. He pointed in the direction of their neighbor's house. "Mrs. Grachek asked us to watch him for a couple of hours."

"Ah." Mattie nodded.

Tom stood and Mattie lifted her cheek for a kiss as chaste as any she had fielded for the past two days from her distant great-aunts. But then, unexpectedly, Tom caressed her arm and said, "I'm glad you're back," and Mattie said, "I am, too," and she was.

The dog caught a ball one of the girls had thrown and then dropped it, attacking the lawn with mock ferocity, tearing at the grass and mud with his claws. Their younger daughter laughed uproariously. The skin of her knees was stained green.

"She seems to be feeling better," Mattie said, and Tom nodded. He sat back down.

"Would you like a drink?" Mattie asked. "I can bring something out."

"That sounds good," Tom said. Mattie went back into the house.

As she stood at the sink, waiting for the pitcher to fill, she watched them from the kitchen window, and in that moment they could have been any family, spending a sunny Sunday afternoon in the back yard. She turned off the tap. Ice, lemons. A tray of glasses and a bottle of vodka.

She didn't want to be out there anymore, playing the worn roles of wife and mother, but still she opened the sliding glass door. She carried everything outside. She smiled and called to them.

SEVERANCE

There was an accident, one afternoon, with the buzz saw. He hadn't gotten enough sleep the night before and took his eyes off the machine for a second.

It was so routine. He'd worked as a carpenter or handyman for more than forty years. This once, though, there was a flaw in the wood, or his hand slipped, and the blade severed his fingers. Things happen so fast, sometimes.

He called his wife from the hospital. She didn't believe him at first. They'd given him a painkiller, and he was a little loopy.

"Peter," she said, and her voice echoed in a way that made him laugh.

She sighed. She was busy, he could tell. Distracted. She asked, "Where are you really?"

"At the hospital," he said, "I swear," but he was choking down the laughter.

Once, years earlier, he had called her from a bar. In the booth, feeding a quarter into the pay phone, he had barely been able to stand upright. She had come looking for him then, and put his arm around her shoulders to help guide him out to the car.

Where was he now? The question haunted him. He fell back against the pillows with the phone pressed to his ear. His mouth was dry.

There was something significant that he had meant to tell his wife.

His hand. The bandages. He couldn't remember what he had already said.

It could wait. But the words came out as another question. It could wait? He felt the urge to laugh again but didn't.

Her voice drifted farther and farther away from him.

Suddenly nothing seemed funny anymore.

"Please don't hang up," he said, and she didn't.

SOUVENIRS FROM ANOTHER LIFE

Exiting the highway one night, a delivery driver fell asleep and rear-ended our car as we sat at a stoplight. He'd been at work all day and was moonlighting. We lived in an expensive city, where it wasn't enough to have a full-time job. The airbag deployed and broke two of my ribs.

One of the things I had always loved about my husband was that he was so big. He could pick me up with one arm. When he squeezed me, I could feel my bones crack.

Now, I shrank and shrank. In the mirror, I could hardly recognize myself. By comparison, my husband was a giant, and every time he touched me I was nearly crazed with pain.

The boy who had driven the delivery truck into the back of our car wrote me letters. Pages and pages and pages of letters. It seemed that he, too, was crazed by grief.

Our baby had died in the accident. The boy had lost his job and was on house arrest until the trial. He was barely twenty-five, with no savings. He couldn't pay rent and ended up living back at home with his mother. Every night, though, he stayed up all night and wrote me letters.

Or so I imagined.

The envelopes continued to arrive day after day.

My husband and I divorced.

I moved in with my mother and stepfather. The letters followed me to the new apartment. I was sleeping in a room that had previously been used for storage, and my old cradle was in the corner.

In the daylight, I knew that it wasn't a cradle at all, but the objects in the room shifted and rearranged themselves in the dark. I saw everything, lying in that room. My ribs had healed months earlier but they, too, ached all night. It should have been yet another phantom pain that kept me up, but on the x-rays, I could see them, spanning the dark shell of my rib cage, glowing ghostly white, as faint as gauze.

My mother had, on the mantel, a portrait of my family, taken when I still had a family. The photographs I found all over the apartment were proof that these things had happened: my courtship, my wedding, the birth of my child. I had, at one time, been a mother.

I threw the boy's letters into the trash without reading them. It wasn't cruelty. I couldn't read them. The words floated off the page, the letters of the alphabet separating and dividing until they could have been a meaningless collection of anything—beads or buttons, even. Anything that, once orderly, had been spilled out into the atmosphere.

The boy had also been a baby, once, and for that and many other reasons I pitied him, and his mother, who during the early hearings had sat behind him in the courtroom and wept, and the judge, who'd had to sit in that room and listen to everyone, and my husband, who had been transformed into a giant but was still powerless in the face of despair, and who had fallen in and out of love as if it were a pool you could dip your legs into and then retreat from when the temperature shifted and everything changed around you.

Or, perhaps, I was the one who had retreated, and yes—that was it.

Many years have passed.

He is remarried now, and the new wife has a baby once a year—fat, cheerful ones, the kind you see in ads—and they are up to six now, and I want to write him a letter, I want to write everyone a letter, and say, Is this the one? Is this the one who makes up for it?

I lie in bed at night sometimes and think about that.

But also, I know him. There's still a hollow there for him, too, and nothing that will ever be able to fill it. Nothing can replace the time when we were young, and our baby slept in the bed between us, in the space that our bodies had made for her.

THE LAWNMOWER

His wife sent him outside, one morning, to mow the lawn. It had been weeks, some of the neighbors were complaining, they'd gotten a letter from the HOA.

It was a Saturday, a sunny day. There were beers inside in the fridge. He was almost done when one of the blades broke. A piece of metal flew out and caught him in the leg.

On the way to the hospital, he lay in the back seat with towels wrapped around his shin. He was teasing his wife, as she drove. If she had just let him relax, none of this would have happened. No one got hurt while sitting on the couch. Ha ha.

She was tense, as she drove, and didn't turn around. She'd left the children with the next-door neighbor.

The wound was deep, but they cleaned it and stitched him up. The bone wasn't broken. A nurse bandaged his leg and sent him home, no harm done.

A week later, they got another letter from the HOA, this time threatening them with a fine. He was still resting his leg, but it seemed to be getting worse. His wife bought a new mower and paid one of the teenagers down the street to finish the lawn and trim back the hedges.

He got a fever. When he went to the doctor, it emerged that the leg was infected. He ended up in the hospital.

They pumped him full of antibiotics and sent him home after two days, and then when things didn't improve, told him to come back. He lay in the hospital bed and stared at the ceiling.

When his wife brought the children to visit, he tried to joke with them. They were bored, though, and just wanted to watch the little TV hanging on the wall. They crowded onto his bed and fought over the remote control.

The infection didn't subside, and finally a surgeon made the call. They were going to have to amputate part of his leg. Good news, though: he would be able to keep his knee.

His wife came to visit, alone this time. Neither one of them knew what to say. She was somber. He wanted things to go back to the way they had been before, when he could jostle her out of a bad mood. Maybe this will save us on socks, he said, but she just put her head in her hands.

When it was all over, he got a prosthetic leg with a metal tube where his shin had been. To make the children laugh, he sometimes took it off and let it sit on its own chair at the dinner table with them. He called it Howard.

They moved to a single-story house. Going up and down the stairs day after day was too difficult for him. The new house was still near the kids' school, but it had a yard full of rocks and native plants, and no homeowners' association breathing down his neck.

The following spring, they drove to Sedona for a vacation. One of the kids wanted to go hiking. They chose an easy trail, and his wife packed up an economy-sized bottle of sunscreen and a box of energy bars.

It was all right at first, but finally he had to stop. He waved the others along. They were all wearing red T-shirts and shorts, and he watched them disappear from view.

The uneven ground was difficult to navigate, and for the first time in a long time, he wished he had crutches again. His stump ached. He sat on a flat rock and removed Howard. Without the children, it didn't seem funny. Just a chunk of plastic and metal.

One hiking boot was laced onto the prosthetic foot. His wife had tightened the laces through the eyelets and around the little hooks. Inside the other boot, on his real human foot, he could feel a blister forming.

He wasn't wearing a watch, and he had to keep getting out his cell phone to check the time. His family had been gone more than an hour. Other tourists walked past holding their cameras. He was sweating, even sitting still.

In the distance, against the backdrop of the red rocks, he saw his wife and kids, in their matching red shirts, round a corner. They weren't alone, though—at his wife's side was a tall, muscular man in a tight shirt and very short shorts. Other hikers overtook and passed them, so they were walking slowly, he could tell.

The children arrived first, bounding up to him like puppies, and the adults followed. His wife's face was flushed. She was carrying the pack, which she removed and set on the ground. "Stand in the shade with Dad," she said, "and I'll get you some water."

To her husband, she said, "Look who I found!"

The man in the tight shorts was someone she'd known in high school, a German exchange student. "He lives here now," she said delightedly, and the former exchange student reached down and affectionately rumpled the hair of the youngest child.

It took a minute to reattach his leg, and everyone had to wait. Tiredness made him clumsy. As they all walked toward the trailhead, his wife chatted animatedly, once even putting her hand on the German man's arm, steadying herself, she was laughing so hard. It had been a long time since he'd seen her like that.

Two of the children were starting to bicker; someone wanted to trade seats when they got back in the minivan. The sun was hot.

As they finished loading up the kids, his wife gave her friend a hug, and the German got into a shiny little sports car and drove away.

"We should get some food," she said. She seemed deflated. Without asking, she walked around to the driver's side so that he could take off his leg. She could always tell when he was in pain.

"Old boyfriend?" he asked, once they were back on the road.

"Oh." She glanced at him quickly. "No."

He watched the mountain scenery slide past the window. "Too bad," he said lightly, "because he is gorgeous."

And then there it was again, her laugh. They both relaxed a little.

He turned up the air conditioning and put on a DVD for the kids. There was no way to know what would happen, was there? A year ago, he had been a different person, and if he was honest with himself, so had she. Everything had changed. Everything would continue changing. All they could do was try to keep up.

FLORIDA, 1993

They flew into Miami at night and decided to go straight to the hotel. They were both hungry but too tired to look for a place to eat. They had rented a white sedan at the airport, and as they drove, Ryan became convinced that another car was following them. Denise had the map, but Ryan kept taking wrong turns, and she couldn't keep up. The car behind them had no trouble, though: it braked and turned and accelerated in tandem with them.

Denise twisted around in her seat, watching out the back window so that when Ryan said, "Where are they now? Is that still them?" she could say, "Yes, yes, they're still there." She didn't know what to do. It was getting dark. They needed to find a police station, she thought, but finally Ryan made a sharp left and the other car kept going.

They waited to see what would happen next. Denise's heart was beating hard, and it was almost a letdown when the car didn't circle back. The whole thing felt unreal, like a scene out of a spy movie. Then they were laughing, shaking, not yet knowing what they'd escaped.

Ryan pulled over and turned on the dome light so she could retrieve the map and find her bearings. The whole way to the hotel, she kept looking over her shoulder, waiting for the other car to reappear, but it never did.

For twenty-five years, if Denise remembers this moment at all, she simply thinks that she and Ryan were the victims of their own imaginations. Then, one night, she is watching a news program on TV and sees an old story about dead German tourists in Florida. After a series of crimes in which travelers were targeted, the state banned rental companies from outwardly marking their vehicles.

At the hotel, Ryan had carried the bags upstairs. There was a big bed. A pool, drinks. They tried to relax.

Once that feeling of paranoia leaked in, though, it slowly poisoned the trip. They argued. After they returned the rental car, Ryan flew back to his wife, and Denise to her husband, as if nothing had happened.

On television, the announcer drones on.

The front door opens, and Denise, still elsewhere, looks up in alarm.

DON'T PANIC

Sutton just meant to tap the back bumper of their car. I mean, he was laughing—we were all laughing. We'd had a couple hits after Sutton picked me up, and everything seemed pretty goddamned funny, if you want to know the truth. We weren't driving anywhere in particular, and Sutton kept passing his house. The curtains were closed, but you could see that the lights were on inside, and I remember wondering what his parents and his little brother were doing while we were outside, driving around in the rain.

We were arguing about whether to head up to this ridge where you could park and look down at the lights of the whole city. What we really wanted to do was leave the car at the ridge and go hang out in the woods, but we didn't want to get soaked. Sutton's stepdad does the weather for channel 11, and Sutton kept saying, "I told you it'd rain," until one of the guys in the front seat said, "Dude, we get it," and turned the radio way up, and Sutton acted like this was the most hilarious thing he'd ever heard in his life.

It was already getting late by the time we ran into Bronson. He'd gotten his hands on his dad's new BMW, and we could see a bunch of other guys from the team crammed in there. Brick was sitting up front next to Bronson, and Brick kept turning around and leaning way over the front seat so that we could see him through the back windshield, flipping us the bird and laughing his ass off.

Sutton kept speeding up and passing the BMW, and as we drove by, we rolled down the windows on the right side of the car and flipped off Bronson and Brick and all of them. We'd won the last game by almost 15 points and we were all feeling pretty good about it. Every time we looped around back toward Sutton's house, though, Bronson would gun the motor and pass us again. After a while, Brick started thinking up new things to do on their way by, licking the glass and mooning us and stuff like that.

We were almost to Sutton's house when he sped up again and got so close to the back of the BMW that I thought we would hit it for sure, but then he slowed down. Brick's face was in the back window, and he was mouthing something at us, but we couldn't really tell what. Sutton edged up to the BMW again, and Brick quickly pulled back into the front seat. The guys in the back of the BMW were laughing at Brick, and we were all laughing, too. Sutton gave the back bumper of the BMW a little tap, and even though it was still raining a little, we could see Brick pretending to get mad, making a face and shaking his fist at us. Sutton laughed and pressed forward again. But this time he must've hit the gas a little too hard, because we jerked forward into the BMW. There was a loud crunch of metal on metal.

Bronson pulled the BMW over in front of Sutton's house, and Sutton pulled up behind him. We all streamed out of Sutton's car. Right away we could see that the windshield of the BMW was broken, and Brick wasn't moving.

Bronson and the other guys were out on the street, too, and Bronson said, "Shit. What're we gonna do?" He kept looking at Sutton, who was standing there in his slacks and white button-down shirt like he was about to deliver the weather to an entire city. Sutton is the one who always knows what to do.

We left the cars parked outside, and Bronson and a couple of other guys pulled Brick out of the BMW and carried him into Sutton's house. Sutton had to unlock the front door, and it was so quiet inside that I thought nobody was home after all, and they'd just left the lights on. There had been a few break-ins already that fall, and everybody was being extra careful. My parents had started leaving the TV on in the living room when they went out to dinner.

As soon as you came in the house, there was a doorway in the wall on your right. It was just a little room where Sutton's mother kept her sewing machine and a bunch of quilts. The guys carried Brick into his mother's sewing room, and Sutton followed them inside and locked the door.

The other guys must've stayed outside, or maybe they just left. All I know is, when Sutton closed that door, I was alone in the front hallway. The house was dark except for the living room, and I practically ran toward it.

There was light jazz on the stereo, and a fire in the fireplace. On any other night it might have been relaxing, but as it was I just paced around the room, grabbing handfuls of my hair and pulling them, repeating "Oh my god, oh my god, oh my god" until I couldn't even understand what I was saying anymore. I tried taking deep breaths but my legs were shaking and I felt weak all over. It was a cool night, but sweat was running down my sides. I just kept pacing and pacing.

I was interrupted by a tiny voice saying, "What are you doing?" It was Sutton's brother, Paul, who was wearing a pair of little Batman pajamas and carrying a blanket.

Fear rose in my throat. If Paul was home, that meant Sutton's parents were home, too, somewhere in the house. I could hear Bronson from behind the locked door, and I knew I had to get Paul out of there. "Hey, remember me?" I whispered. I took Paul's shoulder and steered him back toward his bedroom. "Remember that time I came over and we played touch football in the back yard?"

"Where's Matthew?" Paul asked.

I didn't know what to tell him about Sutton, and I didn't answer.

But the kid wouldn't let up. He said, "Why are you here? Where's Matthew?" in that loud, determined little voice.

"Don't panic," I said, but I was really talking to myself.

"I'm still thirsty," Paul said, and I made him stay in his room while I crept to the kitchen for a glass of water. I had to open the cabinets in the dark, then stand at the sink looking at my own reflection in the window while the glass filled. My buzz had worn off and I was feeling pretty low.

I shut off the faucet. Then I looked up and saw Paul in the doorway. "I'm so thirsty," he said. "I couldn't wait anymore." I just handed him the glass. He took a few big gulps and set it on the kitchen counter.

There was a loud knock at the front door. Paul looked at me, and I looked at him. I couldn't hear anything from the sewing room.

More knocking, louder this time. I grabbed Paul's hand, and we ran through the living room and down the hall back to his bedroom. I closed the door. I tried to lock it, but there was nothing on the handle.

"Where's the lock?" I said, and Paul shook his head.

I could hear shouting now, someone pounding on the front door. I pushed Paul toward the space behind his bed, and when I flopped down on my stomach, he did the same.

My heart was racing. I kept seeing the cars in my mind. Bronson in front of us, Bronson behind. Brick's face in the back window.

Paul had tons of toys and clothes and other crap under his bed, and right in front were two plastic bottles of bubbles. I pulled them out, practically throwing one at Paul. "Come on," I said and opened my bottle, blowing a stream of bubbles into the air in front of his face. Outside the room, there was more shouting, footsteps running. Paul was struggling to get his bottle open. I took it from him and twisted off the cap, pressing the wand into his hand.

"Hurry," I said.

TRIAL & ERROR

At the bar, he had seemed damaged, and maybe that was why she'd taken his hand, turning it over and tracing the lines on his palm, and let him pay for her drink and follow her outside and down the street and up the stairs. He touched her hip, at the door, as she was fitting the key to the lock, and it felt like a scene from a movie—she felt his touch all the way through her body. But inside, things stalled. The apartment was too quiet after the raucous bar, with its loud lights and music and undercurrent of electrical energy, after the noise of the traffic outside—and then when he finally leaned across the couch to kiss her, he upset her drink. There was glass on the floor, in the rug.

She found herself in the bathroom, huddled over the little white pedestal sink with this stranger, unwinding a strip of gauze so thin it was nearly transparent. She wrapped it around and around and around his hand, then up his arm—it was as if, once she got started, she didn't know how to stop—and he said nothing, just watched with those serious, melancholy eyes as she layered the snow-white gauze over itself until the blood-soaked layers were no longer visible, and all the while he said nothing, and it occurred to her to wonder if he could speak English—had they spoken, in the bar, or just touched? She'd had too much to drink and could no longer remember. She looked up, at him and then at their reflection in the mirror on the medicine chest. His hand was probably still bleeding under the bandage, and she felt the urge to kiss it, though that seemed too motherly, and maybe they had lost the momentum anyway and it didn't matter, but just in case, she rested her hip against the sink and leaned forward to kiss him.

They ended up in the bedroom, and in their haste, the lamp was knocked off her bedside table. Her face felt too thick, and there was the business of the clothes—it took too long to get them off, and nothing was going quite how she'd envisioned, or how she would have liked, but wasn't that always the way? His movements were slow and deliberate, and he seemed satisfied with her body. He didn't speak and again she wondered at that. There had been so much talking at the bar, all around her—the revolution of different men leaning toward her to ask a question or say something in her ear, the bartender and his stage patter—yet it all seemed so long ago now, unrelated to the man in her bed. It was just an ocean of sound from another time and place, a past life, and so she closed her eyes and allowed this to happen.

Many years later, at a dinner party thrown by a partner at her husband's firm, she found herself in a little powder room down the hall from the dining room, and it reminded her of her old apartment, and the night at the bar. She'd been suffering over a bad breakup for the better part of a year, she'd been young, it was the first place she'd ever lived on her own. She had been dating her boyfriend since high school, and she didn't know who she was without him. All year, it was a series of missteps, miscalculations, errors in judgment. She read the old letters and cried herself to sleep.

In the mirror, she watches herself applying fresh lipstick. She rearranges the bracelets, smooths down her hair. All of the armor is in place. She barely remembers herself at that particular age, in that particular room, with a kind-eyed refugee observing patiently as she washed and then wrapped his still-bleeding hand in layer after layer after layer of gauze.

MISCALCULATIONS

Only 50 meters separated the house and the stable, which I think he forgot to take into account when he doused the kitchen table with kerosene and struck a match. The pond at the front of the property was stagnant that summer, humming with mosquitos, and as the flames rose, they were reflected in the green water that was still visible between the floating patches of scum.

It had been a hot, dry year, and everything was kindling. He grabbed a garden hose and tried to beat back the fire before it reached the horses; he'd been drunk and miscalculated, or maybe forgotten altogether, but he'd sobered up in the meantime, and he was crying out there in the dark when the fire trucks arrived.

In court, he wore a drab gray suit. His hair had been cut too short and slicked away from the part. The comb marks were still visible. It was either that or bankruptcy, he said, shamefaced.

Six months earlier, a woman in the next county had done roughly the same thing, but first she'd shot her sleeping husband and stuck a lit cigarette between his fingers. The judge was inclined to go easy this time around, on a desperate man whose wife had died barely a year earlier with no funny business, no inflated life insurance policies or mysterious shell casings.

He didn't know what he was doing, the lawyer said, and the man rocked back on his heels. I was in the gallery, close enough that I almost could have caught him. It was shocking to think that we had once imagined sharing a life together, that we had made plans for the future. We had been young, then, but those thoughts had reignited in my mind after I heard about the death of his wife. I had written his phone number on a pad by the phone, but still, for the sake of decorum, it had seemed important to wait.

As he was led from the courtroom, he didn't look up or see me, and it was just as well, because he was no longer the person I had known. That night, I looked out my kitchen window into the darkness. My chest was tight with grief. We had been made small, all of us, by circumstance.

[FALSE ALARM]

He shoves through the doors at the back of the courtroom. In the hallway, he pulls a cell phone out of his hip pocket and calls his parents—first his mother, then his father—to say that the verdict went against him. (He says, "I love you, stay strong," at the end of her call, then turns indignant, almost belligerent, when he makes the second.)

His girlfriend has followed him out into the hall. They don't have to speak; they both know the drill. The calls are quick. When he hangs up, she takes the phone, his blazer, and, as he loosens and slips it over his head, the tie. He unbuttons the dress shirt, pulls it free, and hands that to her, as well, until he is standing in slacks and a plain white cotton undershirt.

Automatically, he turns around and puts his hands behind his back for the guard. The older man keeps his voice low. He says, "It's OK—I can do that inside."

His girlfriend follows them back into the courtroom and emerges a few minutes later alone. She is sniffling, trying to hold it in, trying to get into the elevator and out of the building before it happens.

[STOP]

That morning, arriving at her stop, she saw the northbound light rail on the other side of the tracks, unmoving. It was paused with its hazard lights on—a revelation—but the car she had just departed closed its doors again and continued into the distance. They were opposites in every way.

An ambulance arrived. It stopped in the lane next to the light rail, forcing the traffic to flow around it, and two men emerged with a stretcher. A fire truck arrived—lights, siren, a scream in the cold morning air on the way toward the courthouse.

[SUPERIOR COURT]

Perhaps, in retrospect, it was an omen. She sits outside the superior court and sobs into a handful of napkins from the man with the sandwich cart at the end of the first-floor hallway. When she's gotten it out of her system, she throws the wads of saturated paper into the trash. She wants to go to the bathroom to wash her face, but it's too much trouble to stand in line and go back in past the metal detectors and the guards. Instead, she heads back down the sidewalk toward the light rail.

As she walks, she's trying not to think about what she's going to do now. From the county courthouse down the street, three people emerge, all holding hands—on one end a young groom, in the middle a little boy (also in a suit), and then a bride in a simple white dress, with a rhinestone headband holding back her hair, holding a bouquet of calla lilies in her free hand.

A second woman is walking ahead of them, and she stops in the middle of the sidewalk to turn back and photograph them as they walk toward her. The photographer has her back toward our girlfriend, who stops walking to keep from ruining the photo.

The traffic has stopped for a red light up ahead, and a man in a U-Haul truck honks—two short little beeps—and calls out to the couple. The girlfriend is unable to hear his exact words, but the groom looks both embarrassed and happy and says, "Thanks," and before the traffic starts moving again the bride says thank you to the girlfriend, for waiting for them, for pausing as they take the photograph—and she says, "You're welcome! Congratulations!"—and for a minute she is part of this happier story and she is happy, too.

THE BIGGER MAN

The man went to the pet store to buy himself a little man to keep him company. . . . [He] looked around until in the back he found a cage inside of which was a miniature sofa and tiny TV and one small attractive brown-haired man, wearing a tweed suit. He looked at the price tag. The little man was expensive but the big man had a reliable job and thought this a worthy purchase.

—Aimee Bender, "End of the Line,"
from her book *Willful Creatures*

The man in this story was also big, but he was the kind of man who kept his hands in his pockets to avoid taking up too much space. It was a Saturday, and the animal shelter was open long hours, but he arrived early in the morning. The previous weekend, he'd spent two hours at the pet store buying a bag of kitten chow, food and water bowls ringed with line drawings of cats and fish bones, and a snug little bed. He had just started working from home, and the apartment had never seemed so lonely. He was looking for a pair of kittens who could entertain each other and keep him company.

At last he settled on two small tabbies, a brother and sister: they were both gray with narrow black stripes, but the boy had thick bands of gray on his tail, and the girl had a soft white belly and paws. Still, before he handed the clerk his credit card, the man walked the entire length of the room once more, and in the back, in one of the cages closest to the floor, he saw a little man, about the height of the kittens, sitting on a miniature sofa and watching a tiny, muted television. Like the bigger man, he was wearing jeans and a white button-down shirt.

Mystified, the big man leaned in for a better look, and the little man jumped, scrambling around until he was almost hidden behind the couch, breathing hard.

The big man stepped back. "I'm so sorry," he said.

A shelter volunteer, who was cleaning out one of the cages, said, "Nobody wants that one. Too strange, I guess."

"I think I scared him," the big man said miserably.

The volunteer nodded and said, "That happens a lot. It's skittish."

The big man had only brought one cat carrier for the kittens, so he had to take the little man home in a cardboard box from the shelter. The box had been folded and tucked into the shape of a little house with a handle on top.

He buckled both carriers in the back seat of the car and drove extra slowly around corners. At home, as he unloaded them from the car, he peeked inside the carriers. The kittens were mewing insistently, but the little man was silent. The shelter had kept the miniature sofa and television set, and he was curled up inside the paper box without so much as a hand towel to keep him comfortable.

Over the next week, the big man purchased a large, elaborate dollhouse and began to furnish it with all manner of little furniture, rugs, dishes, and silverware. He found clothing for the little man and a miniature armoire and dresser to keep them in. He found the softest, most comfortable bedding. Having pets was turning out to be more expensive than he had expected, but he didn't mind.

The little man wandered about, testing the various chairs and opening and closing the drawers, looking generally pleased. The big man watched him sitting at the table eating morsels of food, or resting in a miniature wingback chair, reading one of the tiny books the big man had found.

To his surprise and dismay, however, the kittens also admired the dollhouse. They amused each other by batting a little rocking chair out onto the floor, and that night, the big man dreamed that the kitten with the white paws picked the little man up in her mouth and carried him out the open living room window. When he woke, his heart was beating so hard that blood rushed in his ears. The little man was around the same size as the kittens now, but they were growing every day. When they weren't sleeping, they spent their time stalking and pouncing on anything that moved, fraying his curtains or knocking his lamps off the tables.

He worried that they might hurt the little man, and in the beginning he was careful always to close the door of the spare bedroom where he kept the dollhouse any time he left the apartment. But when they were all together, when they watched television together at night, or when he was standing at the counter dicing onions with the little man watching from a kitchen chair, the kittens only wanted to curl up near him and lick the little man with their raspy little tongues, which made the little man laugh, and the big man could not help laughing, too.

The little man did not speak, but he had kind, intelligent eyes, and he listened attentively. The bigger man often read to him, or they sat on the couch in the living room with the kittens and watched the television in companionable silence. The big man loved to cook, and although the portions he made were the same as ever, it was somehow more satisfying to share them with the little man.

Things went on this way for many years. The kittens grew into sleek, handsome cats. The bigger man began to find strands of gray in his beard.

One evening, looking at a magazine, the big man paused over an advertisement for a ready-made cookie dough: a sunny kitchen, a smiling girl sitting at a table, the mother's arm around her. The cookies would be better on a cold day, the big man was thinking, remembering for a moment his own mother, who had died many years earlier; he could remember coming home from school or an afternoon of sledding and finding her in the warm, cozy kitchen with a plate of chocolate chip cookies or a steaming cup of hot chocolate.

He glanced over and saw that the little man seemed equally transfixed, and for the first time, he wondered if the little man might be lonely.

The papers that the animal shelter had sent home with the kittens had been thorough: their date of birth, the reason they were surrendered. There had been no corresponding information about the little man. He had no idea what the little man's life had been like before, how he had come to find himself in a little cage with only a miniature television for comfort. Perhaps he had been part of a family, or—the bigger man thought for the first time—perhaps he wanted a family of his own.

It was an uncomfortable thought, but one that began to trickle out like candle smoke every time he closed his eyes to go to sleep. He had no way of finding out for sure. The little man didn't speak. And even if he decided to move forward, it would be complicated. Where would he even find another little person? And not just any one, but the right one. He turned the thoughts over and over in his mind.

At last, he placed an ad in the local newspaper:

Wanted: Tiny woman. Must be smart, friendly, kind-hearted.

For two weeks, he heard nothing. He had been afraid of teenage pranks, or responses from the merely curious, but he needn't have worried. In fact, he had all but decided to cancel the ad when a woman finally called, late one night, when he was already almost asleep.

They made arrangements to meet at a local park, and the big man arrived early, sitting on the bench nearest the duck pond, keeping one hand cupped protectively around the little man sitting next to him. He couldn't tell how much the little man understood about the meeting—he could be frustratingly inexpressive at times—but when the big woman arrived with her little woman, it was immediately obvious that there was a connection between the two smaller people.

The little man, who had never spoken to him, could communicate with the little woman in a way he couldn't have described; to call it speech seemed inaccurate, but only because it was almost without sound.

In his most hopeful moments, the bigger man had imagined that perhaps the little man would warm to the little woman, and that he would be equally, unexpectedly drawn to the big woman. But she had blunt fingers, stained from nicotine, and a loud laugh that made the two men jump. (The little woman was, apparently, accustomed to her companion's abrasive habits.)

The bigger man would just as soon have left the park and written the whole experience off as a loss, but he could see that the little man was bewitched by the little woman, who had long, silky-looking hair and a soft, melodious little voice, from what he could hear of it. The bigger woman sat too close to him, asking questions in her loud, roughhewn way. Where had he found the little man? How long had he had him? What kinds of things would he eat? Did he keep his area clean? She wanted to make sure that he wouldn't make a mess in her house.

It hadn't occurred to him until just that moment that the woman might not want to separate from her small woman—or worse, might expect him to separate from his small man. He could no longer imagine life without the little man. They were a foursome: the two men, the two cats. He had been willing to adjust to his pet's possible desire for a partner, but he had no interest in merging his life with this unpleasant woman, or letting her take his little man. The thought of it made him feel unbearably sad.

Tentatively, he said, "If they get along, maybe she could come and live with us," but the woman immediately shook her head.

"Oh, no," the woman said. "I could never give her up."

It was too soon to worry about such matters; they had only just met. The big man tried to put it out of his mind.

Although he found the big woman unpleasant, he made every effort to accommodate her schedule. They met at crowded pizza parlors and bowling alleys, and although he never grew to like her, exactly, he no longer minded the long hours they spent together.

Things had settled into a comfortable if not altogether enjoyable routine, so the big man was caught off guard when the big woman mentioned that she was taking the little woman and moving away. Her father had recently died, leaving her a small amount of money, and she had given notice at her job. Rather than selling or renting it out, she had decided to return to live in her childhood home.

The big man was distressed at the thought of separating the little man from the little woman, and he told her so, but the big woman shrugged.

"They'll forget," she said.

It was almost a relief when the woman finally did pack up her belongings and leave. The man had to admit that it was heavenly to have his weekends free again. He no longer had to sit through the terrible movies she liked or feign interest in her endless monologues about her long hours at work, or her painful corns and bunions.

But the little man seemed so wretched. Weeks went by, and he didn't forget the little woman. He fell asleep at night holding a little sweater that she had left behind. He became obsessed with a television commercial for a cleaning product that featured a woman whose face and hair were so like the little woman's that the big man always had to blink, feeling momentarily disoriented. He knew that he would gladly endure any conversation about the big woman's aching feet if it would make the little man happy again.

He asked a neighbor to watch the cats for a few days, and he fashioned a traveling seat for the little man, so that he could have a safe place to sit for the long drive.

The big man had had every intention of ringing the big woman's doorbell and asking to see the little woman, but it was quite late when they arrived. Through the wide front windows of her parents' house, the big man could see a big television set and the big woman marooned in front of it on a giant flowered couch. There was a haze of cigarette smoke in her general vicinity, and he saw her tap the ash from her cigarette into a decorative ashtray in her lap.

He carried the little man around the side of the house, where there was another light on. He stumbled in the dry grass and weeds, which lashed at his ankles, leaving painful stickers that felt like goat's heads in the cuffs of his pants, but he held tight to the little man and continued doggedly through the darkness toward the lighted window.

Inside, they could see a small child's bedroom. The furnishings were old-fashioned but appeared clean and comfortable. And on the floor, sitting up on a doll-sized canopy bed, was the little woman.

The big man could feel the little man's sharp intake of breath. His eyes were wide, and he was almost panting.

Gently, so as not to scare her or rouse the big woman, the big man loosened the hasp and opened the window. He reached in and set the little man on a shelf near the windowsill. Eagerly, the little man scurried down to the floor and ran toward the bed and the little woman, who looked up in alarm and then delight, and all but flung herself into his arms.

The little man held her, then leaned back, smoothing her hair and searching her face with undisguised longing. The little woman was in a short, sheer nightgown, and the big man looked away, embarrassed.

With the window open, he could hear a loud laugh track and the hearty, booming laugh of the big woman. She might never notice if they packed the little woman up in the traveling seat and took her home with them. After a while, it might even be liberating, not to have to take care of someone else anymore.

Inside the bedroom, the little man was kissing the little woman on her cheeks, her lips, her throat. The big man felt a deep pang of regret: the magazine ad, the classified in the newspaper, the meeting at the park. If only he had thought everything through from beginning to end. He slipped away, back down the darkened path toward the front of the house and his waiting car.

It was almost tempting to start the engine and drive away. But he could never leave the little man here forever without so much as saying goodbye, and he knew that there was no way he could do something so cruel as to take the little woman away from the big woman, either. No matter how he felt about her or her decision to leave, in every other instance, he had seen her treat the little woman with nothing but kindness. It was unfortunate, but he found himself all but sutured together with this woman. It couldn't be helped. They would have to work out some kind of mutual agreement.

From the window, he could see the blue light of her television set flickering in the dark, and a light breeze ruffled the grass. He waited outside a little while longer, enjoying the quiet of the night, prolonging the moment before he had to walk up the front steps and knock lightly on the door.

ALL THESE QUESTIONS

When you tell people that you have all boys, they want to know if you tried for a girl. If you are still trying.

Once, in line at the grocery store, a woman said to me, "Why don't you just quit already."

When you tell people that your oldest son is sixteen, they want to know how old you are. If you're as young as you look. When I tell them that I'm thirty-three, I have to look away while they furrow their brows. I know they're thinking it through; they're doing the math.

When you tell people that your oldest son is sixteen and your youngest son is almost a year old, they want to know if all your kids have the same dad. Sometimes they ask outright, which still surprises me, even though it seems like it shouldn't by now. Sometimes all the kids are with me—one with skin the color of café au lait, another with my pale, freckled skin, skin that was the bane of my existence at one point, skin that couldn't hold a tan to save its life—and then people don't even ask. They just look from one kid to another and purse up their mouths.

You might think that a person like Angelina Jolie makes things better, but her family is too public—it's no secret where those kids came from—and anyway, she's an unmarried woman who gets tattoos and holds a gun. The people who don't judge her weren't judging me in the first place.

So I drive home from work at night thinking about the mysteries of genetics and how all these boys look so different even though their father, who left me when I was pregnant with the baby, who finally just couldn't take any more, was always the same man.

I'm driving home early, thinking about how work is the only place I get any peace at all, because when I'm there all people ask me about are window treatments and color swatches, and they don't think about me as a person, as a mother. Without a baby in my arms, I'm as neutral as one of the mannequins in the window of the store next door.

The lights are all off when I get home, and it takes my eyes a long time to adjust to the dark. I don't remember it taking so long, and I don't know—is it because the prescription for my glasses has changed again, or because I am getting older? Is it just a natural change?

This is what I'm thinking about when I start to hear the rustling. In the living room, the baby is standing in his playpen, silent, and my eyes meet his.

The other boys must be asleep in their beds, but the oldest one, Michael, is babysitting. I'm sure he's still awake. And I'm aware suddenly of the scent of the house, which has changed. There's a sweet smell that I know is from his girlfriend, and then of course the rustling coming from his bedroom down the hall.

When I went to work, I left my purse at home by accident, and I'm relieved to see its faint outline on one of the top shelves near the TV, but when I walk closer I see that the purse is open and my old faux leather wallet is open and two twenty-dollar bills are gone. I don't remember whether they were crisp, new bills or whether the paper was worn and faded or even repaired, at some point, with a bit of Scotch tape. What I do remember is that the elderly lady next door gave me exactly forty dollars in cash after I repaired her fence where the posts were falling down, and now the money is gone.

The baby is reaching for me, so I walk into the middle of the living room. I pick the baby up and sling him onto my hip. My heart is beating hard and there is a loose feeling in my hands that I recognize—that fine combination of anger and adrenaline.

At the same time, I am so calm. I am seeing everything very clearly, as if my vision has been shaved down to only the most essential items.

I am picking up the baby. I am walking down the hall. I am knocking on the door of Michael's bedroom.

The rustling stops, and I can hear whispering. He opens the door wearing only a pair of faded jeans. He is much taller than I am, but I stare him down. The light is on in the room behind him and I can see his girlfriend, in a bra and a pair of pantyhose, sitting on the bed behind him. She has her head down and the dark curtain of her hair obscures her face.

"Where is my money?" I ask. "There was forty dollars in my wallet when I left for work."

Michael shakes his head. "I don't know what you're talking about."

"My purse was wide open when I got home."

I can hear my voice rising, and two doors down, on the other side of the bathroom, the little boys' door opens and my six-year-old stumbles into the hall, rubbing his eyes.

"The rent is due on Friday, and we need groceries."

Michael starts to look angry. "I didn't take it. I swear."

Sleepily, his little brother says, "Maybe they needed it for the baby clothes."

On Michael's desk, under the gooseneck lamp I bought him when he was eleven, on top of a pile of papers and unfinished projects, there are three little onesies—a yellow one, a pink one, and a white one with a pattern of tiny pink rosebuds.

I look back at Michael. His girlfriend is still sitting on his bed, chewing one of her fingernails.

I can't stop thinking about the money, the theft. "I know for a fact that I had forty dollars in that wallet," I say doggedly. "The little kids aren't tall enough to reach that shelf. It doesn't make sense that anyone else would have taken it." I pause, thinking. I know that if I think long enough, I will be able to come up with the proof.

QUARANTINE OF THE HOTHOUSE ROSES

Two of the guys on his team had just returned from China, so they were all told to work from home, in a self-imposed quarantine, for two weeks. Scott spent the first three days in his boxers. He slept in, had a beer with lunch. The apartment got too much shade during the day. It was depressing. He was having trouble staying motivated without anyone else to compete with.

He'd been dating the woman in the apartment above his for almost two months. They'd slept together a couple of times, but she still hadn't introduced him to her kids. She got a neighbor to watch them if she wanted to go out with Scott.

She was a dental hygienist. Aubrey. She had long brown hair and brown eyes, and she wore tight blue scrubs to work. Sometimes he saw her on the way to her car.

On the news, the virus was running rampant. Scott's company sent everyone a message saying to work from home until further notice. The schools closed. He'd heard Aubrey's kids upstairs from time to time, of course, but now they were overhead 24 hours a day.

Scott texted her. *Im trying to work*

So am I, she texted back, after 45 minutes.

He walked over to the window. The blinds were closed. He lifted a slat and looked outside. Her car was gone. The damn kids sounded like they were stampeding up there. *You sound like a herd of elephants*, his mother used to say. *Go outside. You're giving me a headache.*

Aubrey got home late, wearing the blue scrubs, carrying a big bag of groceries in one arm and a bag of fast food in the other hand. He waited until he heard her finish putting things away and walk back to her bedroom to change.

U up? he texted, meaning it as a joke, but she didn't reply.

He tried music, earplugs. All day, the kids were bouncing tennis balls and blasting the TV. He didn't know if the neighbor lady was keeping an eye on them or they were just up there by themselves. They were what, 8 and 10? Or younger, maybe. He couldn't really remember.

Scott gritted his teeth. He had a deadline. He took a shower and put on a clean shirt. Pants didn't matter for a conference call.

Aubrey came home in the middle of the afternoon.

Youre home early

She's closing the office, Aubrey texted back, with a sad-faced emoji.

Except for emergencies

But she'll want Lisa for those.

Scott texted: *Wanna come over?*

I can't.

He didn't know what the kids were doing up there. Killing each other, it sounded like. *Lemme know if u change yr mind*

But she didn't. A few days later, he saw her carrying a laundry basket out to her car. He put down his laptop and texted her. *Where r u going?*

Laundromat, she typed back. Tersely, it seemed to him. She squinted in the approximate direction of his window and threw the basket into the back seat of her car.

Whats wrong w/ yr washer

Broken

Call the office, he suggested.

I DID

She spun her car out of the parking space and sped away.

Scott had a washer/dryer combo, too, and he would've let her use them, but she hadn't asked.

The kids were up there doing something again. Jumping from the couch to the coffee table, maybe. He could hear the shriek, then the loud thump, over and over again.

He watched a UPS driver walking around outside, delivering packages. He watched a line of tiny black ants march along the other side of the windowsill.

Aubrey began leaving the apartment less and less frequently. The salons had been closed for a while. Her hair color was fading, and even from a distance, he could see how fried it looked. Dry, frizzy.

While she was gone, he banged a broom handle on the ceiling. The little monsters seemed to interpret the knocking as an invitation to play some sort of game. They began jumping, echoing back the rhythm Scott had used. He became frustrated, banged harder. Bits of plaster scattered all around him.

The weather turned overcast again. Every day for a week, it rained.

The kids seemed to settle down a bit in the evenings, but during the day, never.

Scott was falling behind with his work.

He called the front office to file an anonymous complaint. Even as he dialed the phone, though, he knew that it was probably "anonymous"; he couldn't imagine that the apartment complex didn't have phones with Caller ID. "I'm sorry to do this," he told the girl in the office, but it was a lie.

"Don't worry," the girl said. "You're not the first person who's reported her."

Overnight, someone keyed Aubrey's car. From the window, he couldn't see what had been scratched into it, but he could hear her freaking out all the way from his apartment.

The girl from the front office called to ask him if he was responsible for the damage. Scott was indignant. Indignantly, he denied it. After they hung up, he paced around the living room, stewing. Upstairs, he could hear a series of sharp little barks. Had Aubrey gotten them a dog? Or were the kids pretending to *be* dogs?

The last time he had texted her, he had asked, *Dont they ever go to their dads?*

That was when she stopped responding.

All day and night, it seemed, the kids were barking. He called the office again, but they said there was nothing else they could do.

A few days later, he opened the door for a delivery and found a sign taped next to his doorbell. PLEASE DO NOT DISTURB the sign said in chunky upper-case letters. Underneath was a crude drawing, presumably of him, but even when he took it inside and turned it in all different directions, he still wasn't sure what it depicted.

Scott was laid off via video call.

A few weeks later, Aubrey moved out. He'd heard a lot of commotion upstairs—packing, it seemed now, in retrospect. She backed a U-Haul up to the sidewalk, and the kids helped her carry out boxes.

That night, he lay on the couch in the dark and drank a beer. The apartment above his would be vacant for at least a few days. It could have felt like a victory, but it didn't.

Quiet. That's all it was then. So very quiet.

PORSCHE

Helene decided she'd finally had enough of his shit and left. He got drunk and called her, crying, at her mother's, and begged her to take him back. She felt sorry for him and said she'd think about it.

A month after she moved out, Raymond won the Powerball jackpot.

Helene still hadn't called him back. He bought a Porsche 911 Carrera Cabriolet with a vanity plate that said SHES2L8. He drove the car all over town, parking near her favorite places.

At some point, Helene moved away, but Raymond still drove the convertible with the top down. It was a kind of habit, by that point. Showing her.

THE RAIN
IN BRUSSELS

Outside, in the square in front of the old Brussels Stock Exchange, a teenage girl is arguing with a pair of security guards. We're several floors up in our hotel room, too far away to hear whether she's yelling in French or Dutch, but her body language is unmistakable. We have our own sixteen-year-old girl, back at home.

It's dark already, and raining, but the scene below is illuminated by streetlights. The Christmas market is a week away, and the nearby streets are lined with enormous yellow crates that have yet to be opened. The girl gestures angrily at the guards and begins to shift from foot to foot, weaving like a boxer about to spring. She is with a small group of friends, and two of the boys grab her arms and hold her back.

The men in uniform don't so much as flinch. The girl. She's shouting and throwing her arms, but the boys holding her back are stronger. I'm waiting for the guards to do something—send the girl on her way, yell, put her in handcuffs, anything—but after a while they walk away, not bothering to look back.

The other kids release the girl, and she makes a menacing gesture toward the guards, then paces back and forth, ranting. Tourists passing through the Place de la Bourse with their shopping bags and umbrellas cut a wide berth around the girl and her friends. She's wearing a gray hooded sweatshirt under a jacket, and at one point, she jerks the hood of the sweatshirt up around her face.

Downstairs, in the hotel lobby, on a bookshelf in the area set up to look like a living room, there is a book called *Oog in oog*. When we arrived at the hotel we were so tired that it seemed like a joke. A big coffee table book, white text on a pale blue background. In Dutch, I discovered later, it means eye to eye or, perhaps, face to face.

As my husband stood at the counter, checking us into our room, I sat in the faux living room minding the suitcases and read this title again and again. The book was faced out. On the other couches, there were two young boys, looking bored, whose parents were behind my husband in line, and a woman in an evening gown and impossibly high heels waiting for her date. My eyes scanned everyone in the room and then returned to this big book with the blue cover and the white letters, trying to make sense of them.

The girl in the gray hoodie seems to have worn herself out by this point, may even be crying; it's impossible to tell for sure at this distance, but when I look down again, two of her friends appear to be comforting her. It is still drizzling outside. The rain flicks off the streetlights, making the dark streets shine.

My husband goes into the bathroom to take a shower. He is still suffering from jet lag.

The girl and her friends disappear around a corner. A woman pushing a stroller, and her companion, holding an umbrella, cross the street walking toward us and are swallowed by the mouth of the train station.

In a week's time, this will be another world. The men hanging strings of lights up and down the street in front of the hotel will be finished. The yellow boxes will have been opened, the booths assembled, the Christmas market in place, everything gleaming and laid out for admiration or purchase. Tonight, though, it is raining in the Place de la Bourse.

My parents are probably in their kitchen right now, with breakfast assembled and ready to be cooked. Our daughter is their only grandchild, and they are attentive—indulgent, even. She is on vacation, and if she wants to sleep late, they will not disturb her.

We have just returned from dinner. In a few minutes, we will call our daughter and tell her good morning.

Back at home, the day is still beginning.

EMPTY NESTS

In college, after too many shots, Jackie and a few of her friends dragged a mattress downstairs and into the bed of a pickup truck they had parked underneath the window of her apartment. She was the first one to jump.

Her parents drove all night to get to the hospital. She'd broken both legs. Jackie expected them to be angry, but once they got past their initial concern, they seemed more bewildered than anything else.

Why had she done it? She didn't know how to answer. It had seemed like a funny idea at the time.

They went to the hospital gift shop and bought her gum and copies of *People* magazine. She missed a week of school. Then, after they took her home, another week—until finally she had to drop her classes.

At home, she lay in bed, propped up on pillows, and watched birds at the feeder in the back yard. Her mother brought her tray after tray of soup, as if she were recovering from some other type of illness or injury. No one came to visit. Her friends were all off at college, participating in their own drunken antics, she assumed.

The chickadees and goldfinches flew out of the trees and shrubs, paused to gather birdseed, and returned to their hiding places.

One night, Jackie dreamed of vultures: she was lying on her back on a deserted highway as the birds circled overhead. They could smell the odor of her legs under the casts, she realized, as she cracked open the casts and exposed the carrion underneath, the chunks of rotting flesh between her thighs and ankles.

Her father appeared, saying reproachfully, "Don't carry on like that." He crouched next to her and gestured toward the birds. Not to wave them away, as she had initially thought, but to gather them, to line them up around her. She could hear the sound of their wings rustling as they fell into position. (They were a captive audience, she thought. Or she was the captive, in front of an audience.)

Jackie woke up. As she walked from one room to the next, she noticed that the time was different on every clock in the house. It gave her a panicked feeling, seeing the hands pointing in such different directions.

She woke up.

At last, Jackie recovered. She'd lost a semester of school because of the accident. She took extra classes over the summer and graduated on time.

Thirty years later, Jackie was at work when she got a phone call from the dean of students at her daughter's college. The number was unfamiliar, so she didn't pick up; too late, she recognized the out-of-state area code. She started to shake when she heard him introduce himself in the voicemail message.

Immediately, she was thinking of all the possible catastrophes—the attacks and accidents, the murders and disappearances. Her mind had filed away the details of every newspaper article and sordid episode of *Dateline* she'd seen in at least the past year.

This was her youngest, her only daughter. The boys had been tiny, both still in diapers, when she turned up pregnant again. The girl was the most, the loudest, the wildest of the bunch.

Jackie could have crushed her pelvis all those years ago, or she could have been brain damaged. She was fortunate, someone had told her the night of the accident, that she hadn't broken her neck.

She was alone in her cubicle, and she laid her head on her desk. She was in agony. But then she was calmed, suddenly, by the thought of the man's tone in the message. Some lack of urgency in his voice.

Yes.

Call me back when you have a few minutes.

She could feel herself relax a little.

Jackie sat up. She was an adult woman. She was a mother. She took a deep breath and let it out slowly.

Still, as she called the dean back, she hesitated before she pressed the last button. She thought of her parents driving all night to get to the hospital, and the sight of the street-lights cutting through the darkness as she stood wavering on the window ledge of her apartment. She held her finger over the last button, and then she closed her eyes, and jumped.

THE WRIST CORSAGE

Lucy had spent her whole life trying to please other people, so when he invited her to the Valentine's Day dance, she didn't know how to say no. She and her best friend, who was the head of the party planning committee, had spent hours in her friend's basement, cutting big hearts out of red crêpe paper. There was a blood blister the size of a dime on one of her fingers.

The day before the dance, the whole committee stayed after school and Scotch-taped the hearts all along the hallway leading to the gymnasium. There was one heart for each couple who had purchased a ticket ahead of time. Dutifully, Lucy had written "Lucy & Jimmy" in large, ornate letters on her own heart.

Jimmy picked her up early. He was carrying boxes with matching pink carnations: a boutonniere for himself, and a wrist corsage for Lucy. Everyone complimented Lucy's white eyelet dress, her short shell-pink jacket. Her mother took a photo of the two of them standing stiffly in front of the fireplace. She pinched her mouth and looked watery-eyed at Lucy's father. Lucy looked away, embarrassed.

Inside the school, the lights had been dimmed. The gymnasium was filled with red balloons and lengths of ribbon and red and silver hearts, glittering in the dark.

"Do you want to dance?" Jimmy asked, and Lucy allowed him to take her hand and lead her out into the middle of the floor. Only a few other couples had started dancing, but Lucy was on the committee, and she felt obliged to have fun, or at least to look like she was having fun. She waved at her best friend, who was dancing with her head resting dreamily on her date's shoulder, but Amanda didn't seem to see her.

At midnight, Lucy went to the restroom. Every school dance ended with at least one girl in the restroom crying, so Lucy wasn't especially surprised to find Amanda inside, past the row of sinks, sitting on the floor with her back against the radiator.

Lucy knelt in front of her. "Amanda," she said. "What happened?"

"I think he's using me to make her jealous," Amanda said. Her voice was muffled against her arm.

Lucy knew instantly which girl Amanda meant.

A toilet flushed, and one of the stall doors clattered open behind them.

Lucy reached for Amanda's hands and pulled her up from the floor. The sound of running water was replaced by the hum of a dryer.

Amanda leaned one hip against the last sink. She was crying, and the skin around her eyes was red and shiny.

"Do you want my corsage?" Lucy asked. She didn't wait for Amanda to answer. She pulled off the elastic band and eased the wrist corsage, with its pink carnation, around Amanda's hand.

The girl who had been drying her hands finished and left the bathroom, letting the door swing closed behind her. In the sudden quiet, Lucy kissed Amanda on one cheek, then on the other, the way she had seen on television. Amanda did not look up.

Again, Lucy kissed her on both cheeks, and then she leaned forward and kissed her tentatively on the mouth.

Amanda pulled back a little and wiped her eyes with the back of her hand, sniffing and laughing at the same time. "What are you doing?"

"I don't know," Lucy said.

"You always know how to cheer me up," Amanda said. She put her arms around Lucy and pressed her cheek to Lucy's cheek. Faintly, Lucy could smell her shampoo.

There was a tentative knock on the bathroom door. Amanda's date called in to her: "Are you there?"

Amanda's arms were still around her, their faces close together. "He sounds upset," Lucy whispered, and Amanda did not answer.

She pulled away from Lucy and straightened her shoulders. She dabbed at her eyes with her fingertips. "Do I look okay?"

Lucy nodded, but Amanda was already looking in the mirror hung over the sink, shaking her head at her reflection.

"Amanda?" he called again.

"I guess I should at least talk to him," Amanda said, leaning toward the mirror. She ran her fingers through her hair, patting and tucking. Her cheeks were as bright as apples.

At last she turned and smiled at Lucy, touching her lightly on the arm. "I'll call you tomorrow."

Lucy nodded again, watching Amanda reflected in each of the bathroom mirrors as she walked away, leaving and leaving and leaving the room as if one leaving weren't enough.

WRECKAGE

The new girl returned with a cardboard tray of coffee. She didn't look at Maxwell as she set one of the cups on the edge of his desk.

He turned back to his computer. The words on the screen meant nothing to him; they scarcely seemed like words at all. His desk was in the middle of the office, though, so he tapped and clicked, opening this or that document, trying to look busy.

A few nights past, Hannah had packed the last of her bags and left. She had said she would before, but it had never actually happened. All it took, most of the time, was a promise. Do something, stop doing something else.

The problem he had was not in the promising, but in the following through. Once, he had threatened to kill himself if she left. When he had tried that this time, though—a Hail Mary as she went out the door—it hadn't worked. She had taken everything she owned, and left her key to the front door on the kitchen counter.

He stared vacantly at the computer screen. He opened and closed a series of tabs, typing in nonsense, then slumped back in his chair, exhausted. He sat, looking into space. Lifting his arms was an impossible task. He was a sunken ship, half-buried in the soil and stones on the ocean floor.

At the back of the bedroom closet, on a shelf in the corner, Maxwell found a wooden box Hannah had accidentally left behind. It was fairly large, with a lock that didn't respond when he took a knife to it.

He had thought about calling her, using the box as a pretext, but his curiosity had gotten the better of him. Now, he tried her number. A man answered.

Maxwell was flooded by emotion, some combination of sadness and rage and jealousy, and a sour taste rose up in his mouth. "Is Hannah there?" he managed to say. "I'm calling from the club."

What club he didn't say, she wasn't even in a club, but it didn't matter because the man said, "This is a new number. There's no Hannah here."

This was just the kind of thing a new boyfriend would say, and Maxwell imagined Hannah standing next to this new man, who would of course be taller and better-looking, with a thick head of hair and a sports car in the garage. He would own some impressive sort of house where he always remembered to put down the toilet seat and load his dishes in the dishwasher, et cetera, and he would possess the drive and ambition Hannah thought Maxwell lacked. Maxwell imagined the two of them hooting and high-fiving each other because they'd managed to pull the wool over his dumb little eyes. He couldn't let them know he was on to them, so he just had to say thank you and hang up and let the back-slapping begin. And they were right to make fun of him. He was ridiculous.

The next morning, the new girl put his coffee down on a stack of papers. He would have rebuked her, or at least suggested another option, but there was no point. The coffee girls never lasted long, and if he didn't get back on track, he wouldn't either. He knew that. Still, instead of working through his lunch break, he went outside and dialed Hannah's number again.

The same man answered. He had a pleasant, handsome-sounding voice.

"It's me again," Maxwell said. "From the club. Is Hannah there?"

"Still no Hannah," the man said. "This is a new number, remember?" He sounded cheerful but distracted. Hannah was probably right there, with her hand on his arm.

"Oh, right," Maxwell said. He didn't want to give up too easily. "Well, tell her I said hello." Quickly, he hung up.

The third time he called, the man on the other end asked, "What kind of club is this, anyway?"

Maxwell hesitated. Square dancing, he could have said. Mountain climbing. He was taking too long to answer. All he needed to say was something about books, or fitness, or wine. Films. Jazz. Scuba diving. Some kind of social club. Anything.

Finally, the man hung up.

Maxwell stopped at the hardware store on his way home from work, and before he made dinner, he cut the lock off the box he'd found in the back of the closet. Inside, he was expecting to find evidence. Handwritten letters, a diary. Polaroids of herself on vacation with another man.

That is what he found, but they were nothing to do with Hannah.

He'd been sickened, at first, by the sight of all the evidence. The box must have been left behind by a previous tenant, though, unnoticed by one or both of them as they stacked other items in front of it. When she removed her belongings, Hannah had probably seen it, too, and thought that it belonged to him. It made him sad to realize that she no longer cared enough about him to ask what he kept inside.

He placed the contents back into the box and returned it to the closet shelf. Instead of making dinner, he left the apartment. Aimlessly, he wandered down the darkened streets. If he was lucky, he thought, he would be mugged, or a car would hit him and he would wake up in the hospital with Hannah by his side. She was still his emergency contact. She would be holding his hand and crying, devastated at the thought of going through the rest of her life without him. He would bravely recover from his near-death experience, and she wouldn't suspect a thing because this was so different from his usual machinations.

He liked the idea so much that he even thought briefly about calling her friends and posing as a doctor, but he was afraid they'd recognize his voice. Then he'd be exposed and Hannah would be disgusted with him all over again, when what he wanted was to hold her again and press his face into her neck.

Hannah had a common, nondescript style and short, often shoulder-length brown hair, and as he walked around the city, he kept seeing her—walking in front of him in a short pink jacket, emerging from the back of a black town car, or sailing past him, cool and impassive, in the lighted window of a passing bus. She was nowhere and everywhere all at once.

When he got home, Maxwell called her phone number. The other man answered after several rings. Maxwell himself would have been impatient by this time, he had to admit, but instead the man sounded curious, or so it seemed.

"Hannah again?" he said, instead of hello. "You must be calling from the club."

It was late and he had been drinking, Maxwell could tell.

He was so flippant that Maxwell was offended. This could have been a very serious matter, for all the man knew. Maybe the club was for people suffering from cancer, or addiction, or PTSD. Survivors.

Stiffly, he said, "Yes, as a matter of fact, I am."

"Well, she's not here," the man said.

He must have put his hand over the phone then, because Maxwell could hear him say, "It's that guy again." There was a laugh, also muffled.

Maxwell scowled. "I won't call again," he said, making his voice sound threatening.

The man laughed. "OK," he said. "If you say so."

Annoyed, Maxwell punched the button on the phone and ended the call.

He scrolled through his contacts until he found Hannah's name and number. His finger hovered temptingly over Delete, but then he changed his mind and left her where she was.

The new girl left, alongside his coffee cup, a chocolate chip scone in a slim paper sleeve. She had already turned and was walking away when he called after her to say thank you.

"They're from him," she said, pointing toward the closed door of their boss's office. He was the regional director, a small man with a ready smile. His motto was, Happy employees are loyal employees. He was the one who paid for the daily coffee run, supposedly from his own salary.

Mindlessly, the girl wrinkled her nose to adjust her glasses, which were slipping down her face. Her hands were full.

"Maybe I'll tell him, then," Maxwell said, but he knew he wouldn't. He'd fallen even further behind in his work and didn't want to do anything to draw attention to himself.

The girl walked away, still carefully balancing her tray of drinks. It wasn't the same girl who had been there at the start of the week. That one had had darker features, and hadn't worn glasses.

Maxwell wondered about the endless parade of coffee girls walking past his desk, and if he'd been in a certain kind of movie, the doors along the outer gray walls of his floor might have spontaneously burst open, and the girls would have filed out one after the other in bright matching outfits and performed a choreographed song and dance number involving their cardboard trays of hot coffee, and the blandness of the office would have been transformed at least temporarily by life and liveliness and color, but the image telescoped in on itself and the lone girl continued walking around the room instead, dully distributing coffee and scones.

Over and over again, she continued to wrinkle her face to adjust her glasses. Maybe she had an allergy, Maxwell thought, or a simple motor tic.

She finished and went on to her next job, whatever that was. Maxwell stared at his computer. He had four hours until lunch.

He took a sip of his coffee.

Today could be different. The scone proved it. This could be the day he finally turned things around. His boss would be so impressed that he'd take Maxwell out to lunch and offer him a promotion and a raise.

He answered a few e-mails and entered a series of numbers into a spreadsheet. The phone rang, and he was able to answer a question for a coworker.

When he hung up, he looked at the clock. Hardly any time had passed. His finger hovered over the mouse. He opened a new tab, closed it. There were still more than three hours until lunch. His boss's door was still closed. He sighed and went back to stewing about Hannah.

YEARS LATER (REVISION)

He found himself in a paralytic state. This was the state of Ohio. On a billboard outside—well, if you've been there, you know. Along the highway on his way home from the new job, he had to pass it. He turned up the radio, looked in another direction. Sometimes, though, he was distracted and forgot, and he accidentally looked out the window and saw it dead on.

He's a grown man now, with a wife, and two young children at home. This was another lifetime, with another girl, someone—he thinks now—that he barely knew. They were college sophomores when they found out. They'd been staying up for days at a time, and her father had money, so they were buying expensive stuff. Best-case scenario, the baby would have been born an addict. Worst case, well. You know. They decided not to roll those dice.

The first time he looked up and saw the billboard, he'd been on a high from his first sale at the new place. A fat commission, a pat on the back, the works. He'd been flying down the highway with the windows open and the radio cranked up, and when he saw the sign, he felt like he'd been punched in the gut. He hadn't thought about that in years. Even his wife doesn't know.

Now, seeing it, he feels sick all over again. You just want the bad feeling to go away, you know? He's been sober for years now, and still, he's tempted to stop at a bar. As he gets off the highway, he pulls into a nearby parking lot and into an empty space as if he's in a trance.

It's been a long day. Relief is right there. He can feel it in every square inch of his body.

The neon sign in the window is on. It's orange, and the connection is loose, so it's blinking. On, on, on. Every muscle in his body is tense, he's ready to spring out of the car, but then he doesn't take the key out of the ignition. He can't go back to that time.

Instead, he just sits in the car, idling, watching people walk to and from the strip mall, until his hands stop shaking, and then he throws the car back into reverse and follows his headlights toward home.

Signs flicker past the windows and in the rearview mirror. He's already ten over in a fifty-mile zone, but he knows that no matter how hard he accelerates, he'll still be trapped in the body of the car, unable to reach whatever he's chasing, or outrun whatever it is that's chasing him.

SAVIOR

He left the day after he turned eighteen. He could have gone the day before—the duffel was in his closet, already packed—but she wanted to bake him a chocolate cake, the way she had when he was five or six, when she used to buy him a few comic books and wrap them in tin foil.

She wanted him to blow out the candles. She wanted him to sit still while she cut a thick wedge and set it just so on a paper plate. She wanted. She wanted.

This is what he thought about on the bus, as he stared at his reflection, and at the grasslands shooting past behind it. He couldn't get far enough away.

It was night when the bus pulled into the station. He'd fallen asleep with an old sweatshirt wadded up under his head. It took him a second to get his bearings, and he stumbled a little as he dragged the duffel up the aisle, then down the steps of the bus and out into the semi-darkness. It was late summer, still humid even after ten p.m., out there with the bus's engine still running and the air hot with the smell of exhaust. Moths were collecting under the streetlights.

That was when he had a moment of doubt, but he'd come too far not to continue, so he hitched the bag up on his shoulder and started walking.

It was only two miles. Still, there was a film of sweat on his face by the time he arrived on his father's front porch. There were no lights on, which surprised him; he knocked lightly at first, then louder. He was suddenly afraid that his father wasn't home, and he would have to spend the night outside. His father wasn't the type of person to hide a key under the mat or forgive a broken window.

He knocked again, and this time, the door opened.

His father looked older. He was still short and wiry, with the same muscular arms, the same ragged blue jeans and plain white undershirt, but there were deep pouches under his eyes. He seemed unfocused, and he had to turn the porch light on before he ran his hand through his hair and said, "Oh, Gavin, it's you." He stepped back to let him inside the house.

A girl was sitting on the couch smoking a cigarette. She was older than Gavin, but not by much, he didn't think. Her dark hair was pulled back in a ponytail, and she had a certain type of eyes. They were a light blue, but not the faint, watery color that eyes could be sometimes. They were a blue blue, a piercing blue.

"Where'd you come from," she said. She reached toward an ashtray on the coffee table in front of her and stubbed out the cigarette.

"Home," he said, thinking suddenly of his mother, back in the trailer with her empty box of cake mix.

He wished he could forget her, all her little quirks and habits, the way she pushed his hair off his face when he was hot or the way she would stand at the stove, yelling at him about one thing or another—because with her, it was always something!—and waving a spatula in the air to emphasize her point. She was a waitress, and there was something about food that she seemed to hate. Cooking, cleaning: she hated doing the same things at home that she had to do every day at work. (But she didn't cook at the restaurant, now did she? And then sometimes she wanted to go out of her way to cook for him, like with the cake, but then she'd get mad if things didn't go the way she wanted. When he was around her he felt like he was in the middle of a puzzle that he was never smart enough to solve.)

"Hey!" The girl snapped her fingers at him.

"What a space cadet," she said to his father.

In the kitchen, his father got him a cold Coke. "Where you headed?" he asked.

"Here," Gavin said, wondering if he had misunderstood the question, but his father nodded.

The girl watched as his father gave him a pillow and blanket from a closet in the hallway. "You can sleep on the couch," his father said. "Try not to flush the toilet in the middle of the night. Chrissy's a light sleeper." He put his arm around her as they went into the bedroom.

In the morning, his father made a pot of coffee and poured cereal into bowls. Chrissy made a show of getting an extra chair from a little desk in the nook off the kitchen and dragging it as far away from the table as she could get. She poured herself a cup of coffee and stared out the front window at squirrels or whatever a person could stare at. Gavin didn't care. He had a headache.

"I have to go to the studio," his father said. "We're recording today." He squinted at a wall clock. "If you need to go somewhere, Chrissy can take you. She has a car."

"He can just watch TV like a normal person," Chrissy said. "What do I look like, a chauffeur?"

"He might want to get out of the house at some point."

"Then you take him." She turned to Gavin. "Or walk. You've got legs."

Gavin's father rolled his eyes. "Don't listen to her," he said.

He must have dozed off again, because he woke to a set of keys dangling over his face.

"Earth to Gavin," Chrissy said. She'd brushed her hair and changed into jeans and a T-shirt. "Let's go get lunch. I'm hungry."

Gavin sat up. He felt dazed.

"Come on, Lazy. If you're not outside in two minutes, I'm leaving without you." Chrissy kicked his foot, and he winced as she made contact; her boot had a steel tip. She was already halfway across the room, opening the door, walking outside without looking back.

He got up from the couch and followed her out to the driveway. If he didn't, he was certain that she would follow through on her threat and leave without him, though would that be the worst thing? Mostly, he was afraid his father would be aggravated. (With him? With Chrissy? Or with both of them, for not trying harder to get along? Gavin wasn't sure, but regardless, he didn't want to risk it. If this didn't work out, he had nowhere else to go.)

"Don't touch anything," Chrissy said as he climbed into the passenger seat.

She already had the motor running, and she pulled out of the driveway before he had his seatbelt on. Gavin wished he'd had time to brush his teeth before they'd left.

As they drove, Chrissy lit a cigarette and held it out her window, driving with one arm and letting the other trail out the open window. "If your dad and I got married, I'd be your mom," she said. She laughed: a short, cheerless laugh.

"When we get to the restaurant you should call me Mom. You know, for fun." She stopped at a stop sign. Her left arm was still hanging out the window with the lit cigarette. A kid walking a bike was trying to cross the street, and she waved him across with a lazy flick of her wrist.

Chrissy ordered a chicken sandwich and a Diet Coke to go, and then she watched Gavin eat with an expression somewhere between fascination and disgust.

"Jesus," she said. "Didn't your mother teach you any manners?"

Gavin shrugged, but he stuffed the lettuce back into his burger and took smaller bites.

She gestured to the waitress. "Could we get some more napkins over here?"

The waitress, at a nearby table with a pen and pad in hand, said, "Just a minute."

Chrissy leaned in and said, "What a loser. You'll never catch me working some dead-end job for the rest of my life."

What're you gonna do that's so great, Gavin thought.

Her eyes narrowed. "Come on," she said. "I'm bored. Let's go."

The house looked different in daylight. Gavin hadn't seen it in two years. He was taller than his father now: a tall, skinny kid. The house seemed smaller than he remembered, and more run-down than it had been. It had never been huge—his father had told him that he only stayed there in between tours—but it had been new when he bought it. The whole neighborhood seemed tired now, emptied out.

Chrissy strode ahead of him with her takeout bag. She pushed his blanket aside and settled down on the couch, spreading her food out on the coffee table and turning on the TV.

Gavin wandered around the house, looking at pictures and getting a drink of water in the kitchen. There wasn't much to do. He stared out the window. How had he entertained himself when he'd visited his father? He'd been so much younger. Maybe toy cars, or a coloring book. They'd gone out to eat. Once, when he was thirteen or fourteen, his father had taught him how to shoot pool.

It was just a weekend here or there. Not much more than that.

She'd left Gavin here for a week one time, though, maybe more than a week. He'd been so young that he couldn't remember the details. That time, before she drove away, his parents had had a fight, a bad one. At home that morning, she had packed Gavin's clothes in a garbage bag, and in the middle of the fight, she had picked up the bag and thrown it at his father. They didn't have a bad time, though, after she'd left. They ate bologna sandwiches, and his father took him to his friend Stu's, and Gavin sat on a box in the corner of the garage while the band practiced.

His father came home with a bucket of fried chicken, a pair of six-packs, and $300 in cash, which he fanned out on the kitchen table. "We got a bonus for finishing early," he said.

"It's all white meat tonight, baby," he told Chrissy, and they both laughed.

After they finished eating, he and Chrissy washed their hands at the kitchen sink and moved over to the couch. Chrissy had just finished watching *Divorce Court* and the afternoon talk shows, but she curled up next to his father, pulled Gavin's blanket over her legs, and settled in to watch a rerun of *Die Hard*.

Gavin finished his drumsticks and coleslaw. "I'm going for a walk," he said.

His father grunted without taking his eyes off the screen.

The only other person outside was a man walking a dog the size of a small horse. Gavin moved aside to let them by. He put his hands in his pockets. There wasn't anywhere he needed to be.

When he woke up the next morning, his father had already gone back to the studio. Chrissy was sitting at the kitchen table with a mug of coffee. Two slices of toast, burned black, were on a plate on the counter.

"That was the last of the bread," Chrissy said. "If you want some, you'll have to go to the store."

Gavin cleared his throat. "I don't mind," he said.

She didn't answer, or look up when he left the house.

He bought bread, milk, a bag of oranges, and a lottery ticket. On the way back to the house, he was in no hurry, and he took a circuitous route, winding his way through the neighborhoods. He was turning from one street to the next when he heard voices.

A few white pickup trucks were parked in front of a construction site. He could see his father, talking to a man he'd never seen before, and Stu, carrying a pile of boards into the open space where the front door of the house would be.

Instinctively, Gavin stepped back. He retraced his steps and bypassed the site, walking toward his father's house as fast as he could.

Chrissy was still at the kitchen table where he'd left her. "Took you long enough," she said, and got up to carry her mug to the sink.

Gavin was having trouble catching his breath. "Where's my dad's guitar?" he asked.

"I don't know," she said. "In the bedroom closet? What do you care, anyway?"

She went in the bathroom and closed the door.

He stood alone in the living room. The milk was sweating, and he put it in the fridge. He threw the bag with the other items onto the counter.

His father came home late, drunk. "I did not win at cards tonight," he said, and Chrissy rolled her eyes.

"Do you ever?" she asked.

She bent down to unlace his shoes.

Gavin watched her help him into the bedroom.

In the middle of the night, the bedroom door opened. Gavin was asleep on the couch, and the sound woke him.

Chrissy came out of the bedroom wearing a short red and orange kimono. She walked into the kitchen, her bare feet almost soundless as she crossed the floor. Gavin heard the refrigerator open, and she walked back through the living room carrying a wine bottle and two empty glasses.

She must have had a napkin, too, because she dropped it as she walked through. Gavin could see the white paper flutter in the dark.

Quietly, she put the glassware in the bedroom and came back out for the napkin. As she leaned forward to retrieve it, the kimono fell open a little, exposing the swell of her breasts. She looked up and caught Gavin's eye.

She stood up and pulled the sash tight against her waist. His cheeks burned.

He turned toward the back of the couch and shut his eyes. The door closed again.

A little while later, there was rustling, then the creak of a bed. The sounds were soft at first, then louder. From the other room, he could hear Chrissy panting and moaning.

Gavin put his pillow over his head and tried to think about something else.

Had it been a dream? He wasn't sure.

It was daylight again. Someone was moving around in the kitchen.

He got up. It had been a hot night, and he'd kicked off the blanket. He'd slept in a clean pair of boxer shorts.

The door of the bathroom was closed. Gavin could hear water hitting the shower stall.

He stood in the hallway, waiting.

The water stopped. A towel was pulled off the rack. Gavin heard the snap of the medicine chest, then a drawer sliding back and forth. He went on staring at the bathroom door.

When it opened, his father was in blue jeans and a light T-shirt with a square of darker colors in the middle. The fabric strained over the muscles of his arms. He was so much shorter than Gavin now. He paused in the doorway.

Gavin was standing there, waiting. His father reached out and pushed him hard in the chest. It knocked him back against the wall.

For a second, Gavin couldn't catch his breath.

"You think you're such hot shit," his father said, "but I could still take you." Gavin shrank, waiting for another blow, but his father strode past him and down the hall instead.

Gavin stood outside the bathroom. The door was hanging open now. There was still steam on the mirror over the little porcelain sink. His hands were shaking. His arms, his legs.

Inside, he was a ghost, empty. But then the fog lifted. In the mirror, his face looked the same as before.

He had $200 in a Band-Aid tin in the bottom of his duffel. After he heard the front door close, he packed up and left.

On the way to the bus station, he stopped at the construction site. His father was up on a ladder. Gavin called to him.

"I'm going," he said. The only other thing he could think to say was, "Thanks for the fried chicken."

This elicited a grudging laugh. His father laid his tools on the scaffolding and climbed down the ladder.

"You take care now," he said. He clapped Gavin on the arm.

What happened? Gavin wanted to say, but he didn't. The man standing in front of him was someone he didn't know.

They both nodded; then his father climbed back up the ladder. Gavin hiked the duffel up on his shoulder and turned away. On the way to the station, all he could hear was the sound of his footsteps.

That morning, Chrissy had opened one of the kitchen windows. He found her sitting at the table, smoking, looking pensive.

"Bye," Gavin had said uncertainly.

He couldn't have said why, but at the last second, he felt guilty about leaving her there alone.

She didn't look up. She raised her hand in his direction— a dismissive wave—and took a drag on her cigarette, blowing a stream of smoke through the pores of the window screen.

FUGITIVE

Gavin stumbled on his way down the steps of the bus. He reached out to catch himself, sandwiching his duffel between the side of his body and the pleats of the door, which smacked aggressively against each other. Gavin straightened, pausing a moment before he stepped out onto the ground. The woman behind him shoved a tip of her suitcase into his back. "Move it along," she said. "We ain't got all day."

Outside, the sun gave off a harsh, exposed glare. He'd been asleep on the bus. His head was already pounding, and he could feel a slick glaze of sweat on his forehead.

He hadn't had a shower in two days. He hadn't spoken to his mother since he got on a bus on his way out of town, though, and the last thing he wanted was to go home. Before he left, he'd sworn he would never come back. He felt tired thinking of that, and old: the bravado he'd felt as he stalked away from his mother's trailer was a distant memory now.

Still, instead of turning in her direction he went north, toward Sara's house.

As he walked, the gravel alongside the road was replaced by sidewalks, the cars up on blocks by decorative fences and flower borders. Gavin slowed. It was cooler here, and he relaxed a little, slipping through dappled light under a canopy of shade trees.

Her house was modest but inviting. It was set back from the street, tucked amongst the foliage, and Gavin hesitated a second before opening the gate. At the top of the steps was a wide front porch with a pair of plantation-style rockers.

There was a time when he and Sara had sat outside in these chairs. Now, he rang the doorbell like any stranger.

His heart was beating hard. He could hear footsteps, then a long pause as she looked, as she always did, through the peephole. When she opened the door, Sara gave him a withering look. "Oh, great. It's you again."

He had put his arms out toward her—a wild miscalculation, he saw now—and he blushed.

"Oh, come in already before the neighbors see," Sara said, stepping aside and then closing the door behind him.

Sara's mom and stepdad were both family doctors. They worked at a free clinic they had started downtown. Sara wasn't supposed to have friends over when she was home by herself.

In the kitchen, she gestured toward the table and chairs and, in an act of mercy, poured him a tall glass of iced tea.

She slid into the seat across from his. "What're you doing here?"

"Looking for you," Gavin said.

Sara raised her eyebrows. "Well, aren't you thoughtful."

Her parents seemed equally ambivalent about Gavin's return. That night at dinner, her mother said, in a polite tone, "Now, why can't you go home again?"

An awkward silence settled over the table. Her parents hadn't seemed to mind that he was in the house, when they arrived home from the clinic in their scrubs. Earlier, Sara had let him use the shower, and they were in the kitchen cutting vegetables for dinner. She was older now — she'd turned eighteen while he was gone ("I appreciated the card," Sara had told Gavin sarcastically) — and her parents had started to give her more freedom.

She looked older than when he had seen her last, too: her hair was a little shorter, just past shoulder-length, and cut in a loose, flattering style. A couple of months earlier, she had graduated from high school and gotten a job as a bank teller. "I usually wear a suit," she had said at the kitchen counter, looking down at her jeans, "but it's my day off."

Sara was a pretty girl, but not showily so, and he could imagine her standing behind the cutout that would separate one station from the next, in a smart suit jacket, counting out money.

"Do you want to?" Sara asked. She looked irritated.

Gavin looked around the dinner table at her parents. They were studying him with interest.

"I thought you said you didn't have anywhere to go," Sara said. "You don't even have a car. Where else are you going to sleep, the street?"

He didn't know how to answer. The plan, if you could call it that, had ended at Sara's doorstep. It never would have occurred to him to ask if he could stay, or that if he did ask, they might say yes.

"Maybe for a few days," Gavin said. "If that's all right."

When the two of them were alone in the living room, before he went upstairs for the night, her stepfather said, "No funny business."

Sara's parents had hung a string of little bells across the doorway of her bedroom, he said. Their bedroom was just down the hall from her room, and they were both light sleepers. Her stepfather pointed his finger at Gavin and pulled an imaginary trigger.

Then he smiled faintly, just enough to show that he wasn't this guy—this caricature of a bloodthirsty father who would go to any lengths to protect his daughter—and Gavin nodded uncomfortably, trying to return the non-smile.

If only Sara's stepfather knew how angry she was, and how unlikely any liaison would be; then they could forego this entire uncomfortable charade. (Sara hadn't even made up the sofa bed: she'd practically thrown a pillow and sheets at him.) But Gavin just said, "Yes, sir," because he didn't think it would be wise to elaborate.

Every morning, after Sara and her parents had left for work, Gavin folded his bedding, pulled himself together, and went job hunting.

It was hot, even in the shade. He wandered around looking for Help Wanted signs, haunting the places he remembered from before.

Gavin and his mother had moved here when he was fifteen—a tall, skinny kid with a leather jacket and the equal parts swagger and insecurity that came from mistakenly believing that he was the son of a rock star. Gavin had been a year ahead of Sara in school. She was good at math, though, and they ended up in the same class.

Sara's father had died in a machine shop accident before she was born. Her mother had married her stepfather when Sara was five and they were both halfway through medical school. Sara had spent much of her childhood with her grandparents, who lived nearby.

The town was small enough to be stifling but too big to be welcoming. The locals had extended networks of family; they'd grown up being taught by their parents' teachers, in the same classrooms with their cousins. They didn't need anyone else.

And though Sara had grown up there, too, her parents were busy trying to keep a business afloat, and her grandmother rarely left the house. Sara never had the backyard pool parties her friends described when they came back from summer break, where aunts and uncles converged with covered bowls of potato salad and watermelon, and the kids swam while the adults sat on lawn chairs and gossiped and drank beer and barbecued.

Gavin's mother was a waitress, a woman who spent all day on her feet, taking care of other people, and by the time she got home, she just wanted to be left alone. Every ounce of restraint she had was used up at the restaurant. She hated cooking and food and him, it seemed, for needing nourishment. At night, she stood at the stove, brandishing a spatula and yelling at him about one thing or another.

He sat next to Sara in class. They both felt like misfits, and they were too young to realize that at that time in their lives, almost everyone else did, too, in one way or another. They clung to each other for two years.

Gavin walked past the restaurant where his mother worked. It was a diner, really, with an awning and wide glass windows all along the front. In the late afternoon, when the sun was low, there were thin sun shades that she could pull down if someone complained about the glare.

Inside, he knew, he could get a sandwich, fries, and an ice-cold Coke for $6.99. His stomach was growling. Still, he crossed the street and kept on going.

When he woke up, everyone was already gone. A pair of half-eaten crusts were on a plate next to the kitchen sink.

Gavin loaded the dishwasher and wiped off the table. He was tired from the day before. Sometimes, after job hunting all day, he'd follow his mother home, or around town as she did her errands. Stopping at the grocery store, for example, or at the post office.

He wished he knew what she was thinking. It was strange—when he lived with her, he thought she'd never stop telling him what she was thinking. She was angry, or bitter, or (occasionally, when she'd had too much to drink) sentimental.

It was her day off. Gavin sat in the mottled patch of shade under a gnarled, anemic old tree in the abandoned lot across the street, watching for her to come outside.

The trailer looked the same. Small, claustrophobic.

When she finally left, he gave her a couple of minutes to get ahead before he rose and brushed off the seat of his pants.

Every day of his life with her, it seemed, he had wanted to escape. Now, watching her back as she disappeared behind the automatic doors at the CVS, well—he didn't know why, but it gave him a pang.

On his way back to Sara's, Gavin bought a carton of eggs, some ripe strawberries, and a lottery ticket. He was down to his last couple of twenties.

The night before, Gavin had told Sara that he wanted her back. He interpreted her silence as interest, but when he leaned forward, trying to kiss her, she turned her face coolly aside.

Here he was again, always miscalculating.

At the park near her house, he saw two teenagers lying entwined under the trees. One summer, Sara had packed a picnic lunch and taken him there. All afternoon, they lay on a blanket under the trees. He was afraid someone would see them and report back to her parents, but they'd escaped notice—or, at least, they both thought they had.

This had been during a lull. Later, when the fights with his mother turned more vicious, Gavin paced the floors of the trailer like a caged animal. He hated everything here— the town, the house, her unpredictability and anger. He became fixated on the idea that his father could save him from all of this. Gavin could tour with the band, do odd jobs; they could make up for lost time.

He graduated from high school and abruptly broke up with Sara. The day after he turned eighteen, he left town and took the bus straight to his father's house. The duffel had been in his closet for days, already packed. The thought of escape filled him up like a drug.

But then his father had turned out to be more of the same: an intermittent construction job, a drinking problem, and a dead-eyed girlfriend with a mean streak. Which was the fire, and which was the frying pan?

Gavin had left his father's house with $200 in cash in an old Band-Aid tin hidden in the bottom of his duffel bag. He went to Chicago to stay with a guy he knew from high school who was renting a room and waiting tables while he tried to break into advertising. For over a year, Gavin washed dishes in the back of a Thai restaurant and slept on a mattress on his friend's floor.

Then one night when he went to put away his tips, he discovered that all of the money he'd saved was gone. His friend been taking pills for a while, but it had mostly been a low-key addiction. Gavin didn't wait for him to come home. The next morning, Gavin went by the restaurant to get his last paycheck, paid the landlady what he still owed on his half of the rent, and headed toward the bus station.

Two hours before she should have gotten off work, Sara showed up at home. She sat down next to Gavin on the couch. Earlier in the afternoon, she and one of the other tellers had been held up at gunpoint. She was still shaking. The guy had been wearing a ski mask and gloves. He'd gotten away with almost five thousand dollars.

She grabbed Gavin's arm. "Please don't tell my parents," she said.

"Why?"

"They'd make me quit."

"Shouldn't you?" Gavin wanted to say, but didn't.

For the briefest instant, he was grateful to the gunman for this warm hand on his arm, and then sick with shame and fear and dread at the thought that something could have happened to her, or that something could still.

Dinner was quiet. Sara's stepfather was out with friends, and Sara's mother had a bad headache. She took a sleeping pill and went to bed early.

Gavin was lying on the couch, not quite asleep, when Sara snuck downstairs. "Do you mind if I lie here with you?" she whispered.

He moved toward the back of the couch to make room for her, and when she lay down, he put his arms around her.

Sara relaxed against him. He was suddenly aware of her skin, and the thin layer of silk or satin under his arm. His heart was beating so hard he thought she must be able to feel it. She turned over and kissed him, sliding his hand under the hem of her negligée.

Then, in the middle of things, they heard the door. Sara froze.

Gavin was still inside her—she was on top, with his hands on the small of her back. She leaned forward, holding him close with her face against his neck.

It was late, and dark in the room. Her stepfather dropped his keys on the floor, then bumped lightly against the wall.

"Shhhh. . . . Don't wake him up," he mumbled.

Gavin heard his footsteps as he shuffled up the stairs and down the hall to his room. The house turned quiet again.

"That was close," Sara breathed. She sat upright and looked down at Gavin. She ran her fingers through his hair, and started moving slowly against him again.

Gavin felt the couch shift as someone sat down next to him. He opened his eyes, still half in a dream.

In the early morning light, he could see that Sara had showered and dressed for work. At some point in the night, she must have slipped back upstairs.

She leaned down, in her freshly ironed blouse and suit. She leaned down, and he kissed her goodbye and sent her off to a possible death, as he did every day.

When the house was empty, Gavin folded the bedding in a neat pile, packed his duffel, and left. There was no way he could sit across the table from her mother and stepfather night after night eating their groceries and answering their questions.

With the bag slung across his back, striding across town, he almost felt like himself again.

The night before, sitting on the couch with Sara, he hadn't told her that he'd finally gotten an offer, though the job wouldn't start until the following Monday. He couldn't wait to have money in his pocket again.

He walked past the strip mall where the bank was located, looking for anything out of the ordinary.

A patrol car was parked in the shade by the far corner of the parking lot, mostly hidden by a pair of minivans. Sara's coworker hadn't been able to throw a dye pack in with the cash, but the getaway car had been visible on the bank's security footage. The police were optimistic about catching the thief.

Outside the restaurant, someone had looped a dog's leash around the railing. The dog was sitting on the sidewalk, and as Gavin approached, the dog got up and walked toward him. It was a friendly-faced beagle.

Gavin crouched down and stroked the dog's head. He wished he could untie it, or unclip the leash and let the dog run free in the world, but he didn't. He scratched gently behind its ears and left it tied up there under the overhang.

Tilting its head to one side, the dog considered Gavin as he stood up, lifting the duffel back onto his shoulder.

"Wish me luck," Gavin said. He pushed through the swinging glass door of the restaurant and went inside.

The beagle stood outside at the window—watching attentively as Gavin walked toward his mother—but the door had already swung closed behind him, and it wasn't possible to hear whatever he said next.

THE BODY IN THE BEDROOM

On our first anniversary, as we were sitting down to dinner, there was a knock at the door. We were working, that summer, as the managers of an apartment complex. My husband was a bit older than I was and used to taking charge. He was the first one to get up from the table.

At the door was a kindly man in his early seventies. Our apartment was small—little more than a living room-slash-eat-in kitchen and the bedroom—and he apologized for interrupting our meal.

He and his wife had been expecting one of their neighbors for breakfast, but she'd never showed. Tonight, after calling repeatedly, they'd gone over to knock on the door of her apartment. There'd been no answer.

Their friend's bedroom was also along the wall of the outer walkway, though, and her blinds were askew. Through the window, this man had seen her lying, unmoving, in bed. Even when he tapped on the window—first quietly, then with more urgency—she didn't stir.

We had a master key. I blew out the candles and followed the two men outside and up to the woman's apartment. As we walked past other apartments, I could smell other dinners cooking. Faintly, briefly, we heard a baby crying before being soothed somehow.

My husband was the one who knocked on the woman's front door, then the bedroom door, then went in. He felt unsuccessfully for a pulse. He found a telephone hanging on a wall in the woman's kitchen and, after calling 911, remembered to call the owner of the apartments. He's always been the type to keep a cool head.

The man who'd come to find us went home to his wife, who was a few doors down in their apartment, inconsolable. The EMTs came and left. Then, during the long wait for the coroner, my husband left to take care of some detail I can no longer remember.

This was a long time ago. I was twenty years old, alone in the apartment with the body of a woman I had never met in life.

It was not the first time I'd seen a dead body—it wasn't that. It was more about the fact that I didn't know her. It felt oddly, excessively intimate.

We were alone in the apartment for a while, just the two of us. The layout was similar to mine, and I stayed in the living room, not sure what to do. There were magazines on her coffee table, but I didn't pick them up. Even if the person you're waiting with is a stranger, there's not much you can do, or feel OK doing, while waiting for a coroner. Nothing feels right.

Two men arrived with a stretcher. The dead woman was zipped into a thick black body bag and taken away. Later, we found out that she was scheduled to have heart surgery the following week. She was terrified and just wanted to enjoy her last few days before the operation—planning meals with friends, signing up for a painting class. She seemed to have died peacefully in her sleep.

Later that night, when my husband and I returned to our apartment, we were gentle with each other. As you might imagine, the moment was lost, so we didn't look for a matchbook and light the candles again. Still, we sat back down in front of the linen tablecloth and flowers and ate the cold food, because no matter what happens, the living tend to go on being hungry.

Somberly, we undressed and climbed into bed. We were young then, and had no money to speak of. The dinner had been the extent of our plans.

Earlier that day, during office hours, I'd answered the phone at our desk in the lobby. An older woman and her husband had just moved into an apartment on the fourth floor. The previous owner had left behind a pair of twin beds in the single bedroom, and she wanted to know if we could come up and push them together.

I sent my husband upstairs. He was dutiful man. He pushed the mattresses together so that the elderly wife could lie in bed with her husband.

That night, we lay close together, without speaking. It was still our anniversary. Everything that had happened felt like an omen. Good or bad, though, I wasn't sure. What did all of this mean for the future?

We were just two people, still warm and living, on this earth.

In the middle of the night, I woke, and I could see his profile, a faint outline in the darkened room. We were in an ocean of silence. Softly, I touched his cheek, and he went on sleeping.

FOUR-IN-HAND

Andrea's father liked to walk her to school. Though he would stop back at home before leaving for the day, he was already dressed in the crisp slacks and button-down that he wore to work. Her mother knotted his tie and smoothed down the collar every morning. He had lost an arm in Vietnam, and the empty sleeve was always folded neatly and pinned against his bicep.

Sometimes, after the dinner dishes were dried and put away, Andrea's mother would set up the ironing board in front of the television. She liked comedies: *The Cosby Show, Family Ties, Who's the Boss?*—sometimes *ALF* if she was in the mood. She would watch *Cheers* or *Three's Company* in a pinch, but she preferred the family shows.

If Andrea had finished her homework and drunk her milk without complaint, then she was allowed to watch, too. Her mother had removed her apron after dinner, and she stood in front of the TV in a lightweight dress and her house slippers.

First there was a hot bead of water sizzling on the iron, then the scent of the clothes. Andrea liked to press her hand against the cotton while it was still warm.

It was dark outside, a crisp fall night. Her father sat at his desk in a circle of lamplight, going over a stack of papers. Andrea got a quilt out of the hope chest in her parents' bedroom, and she curled up on the couch.

The room filled with the sound of the laugh track, but no one looked at the television and none of them laughed. Her mother was flushed from standing over the stove, then the sink. Andrea watched as she set down the iron and rubbed the back of her wrist across her forehead. Her mother had a scar on the inside of one arm where she had rested it against the handle of a Dutch oven and burned a long pink crescent shape.

Andrea didn't know why she always returned to this night. The lamp, the quilt, her mother's arm.

The next morning, her father was leaving on a business trip. That night, Andrea sat on the bed and watched her mother pack.

She folded the shirts and slacks and laid them in the suitcase. Standing in front of the mirror, one by one, she looped his ties around her own neck, then gently loosened the knots and lifted the ties over her head. She wrapped them all in tissue paper and placed them into his suitcase.

A taxi arrived early to drive him to the airport. Lights slid across the front windows of the house; car doors slammed outside. He was already gone by the time Andrea woke again and went down to the kitchen for breakfast.

Andrea's mother usually stayed at home in the morning. She kissed Andrea goodbye and stood at the door waving as they set off toward the schoolyard; she must have carried her dishes to the sink a million times as she waited for her husband to return for his second cup of coffee before continuing on to work.

Without him there, the machinery broke down. Her mother was still wearing a bathrobe when it was time to take Andrea to school, and instead of going upstairs to change, she slipped on a pair of shoes and went out to the garage in her nightgown and robe.

Uncertainly, Andrea followed, carrying her book bag, and climbed into the back seat of the car.

Her mother put the key into the ignition and started the engine. The radio was playing too loudly. Andrea hadn't slept well the night before, and her head hurt.

They were already backing down the driveway when she remembered her math homework, still inside on the table. She had written the problems neatly and showed her work and circled the answers, the way her teacher liked, and she couldn't leave it behind; she had to run back inside even though now they were really going to be late.

Her mother was muttering as they drove toward the school, the specific words drowned out by the music, but Andrea knew she was upset about the pink slip, about having to go into the office and sign Andrea in. They were almost there when they saw the girl on the bike hit a rock or a crack in the sidewalk and go down.

Andrea's mother pulled over, yanking up the parking brake. She hurried over to the girl, and Andrea followed. The girl was crying, and Andrea couldn't understand anything she was saying. Blood was gushing out of her head.

Run to the school, Andrea's mother said. Tell them to call 911. She pulled off her bathrobe and knelt, next to the girl, in her white eyelet nightgown. She pressed the robe against the girl's cut.

Andrea ran. In the office, her heart was pounding so hard she could barely get the words out. There were spots in front of her eyes. She had to catch her breath before she could go back, with the school nurse jogging alongside her.

Her mother was still kneeling next to the girl, blood on her hands and the sheer white nightgown, and Andrea wondered if this was what she had looked like when Andrea's brother had died, when Andrea was too young to remember.

Sirens cut through the cold air, and the girl was loaded into an ambulance. The blood-soaked bathrobe belonging to Andrea's mother lay on the ground. They stood on the sidewalk watching the police and firefighters and everyone drive away.

The street became still and quiet again. A row of birds lined up on a light pole and peered down at them.

They got back into the car and drove home. When Andrea was home sick, her mother would draw her a bath and make soup and tea, and so Andrea went into her parents' bathroom and started the tap.

Her mother came out in clean clothes, with her hair combed. They lay next to each other on the couch. Andrea pressed her body tightly into her mother's side. All afternoon, they remained together, half-watching reruns of *I Love Lucy* and waiting for her father to come home and bring them back to life.

AROUND HER NECK

Stacy woke up in the hospital. A nurse was turning on the light, getting ready to stick a thermometer under her tongue and take her blood pressure. It was the middle of the night. The new baby was asleep in a plastic bassinet next to her bed, and Stacy had just drifted off. Or she thought she had, but it was hard to be sure of anything in here.

The nurse switched off the overhead lights, and Stacy dozed off again. Twenty years earlier, on her way toward the elementary school, she'd gone over the handlebars of her bike and landed on her head. It was the first time she'd ever been in a hospital. She woke up in the middle of the night and saw her mother, asleep on a cot under the window.

They had just moved. Her mother, freshly divorced, had a new job. She needed to be at work by 7:30 every morning, so it was Stacy's responsibility to make herself breakfast and get to school on time.

This was easier said than done. The bike she'd been riding was a garage-sale find that had once belonged to her brother, and the chain kept falling off. Stacy had been late three times already, and the woman in the office had warned her that if she got another pink slip, the principal would call her mother in for a meeting.

The morning of the accident, she'd been watching television, which her mother didn't allow before school. But her mother wasn't there, was she? Stacy just wanted to see a few minutes of *Captain Kangaroo*, and her brother had already left the apartment. She got home before he did, too, and she had a key that she wore on a lace around her neck. Every day at school, Stacy kept it tucked inside her shirt where no one could see it.

Their father thought that she was too young to stay home by herself, but it was only for half an hour at a time, or a few hours on the afternoons that her brother had soccer. She already knew how to use the stove, and really, what could go wrong?

In the hospital, all the next day, her mother sat in a chair next to her bed and patted Stacy's hand and cried. The job was so new that her mother's insurance hadn't kicked in yet. The ambulance ride alone was going to cost them an arm and a leg.

After she'd been thrown from the bicycle, Stacy had lain on the ground and opened and closed her eyes. It was like being underwater. Her hair was sticky with blood. A beautiful woman in a white dress knelt next to her and held her head until the ambulance arrived.

Stacy woke with a start. She had been dreaming of the woman in the white dress, a dream she remembered vaguely from the years after the accident. She put her hand on the baby's skin to make sure that she was still warm. During the delivery, the umbilical cord had been wrapped around the baby's neck. She had been blue when she was born, and a neonatal team had rushed into the room and revived her.

It had taken Stacy a minute to realize what was happening. She hadn't registered the baby's silence, at first. She had been smiling at her husband, relieved, the pain abated at last, and she had said, Where is she? and when her husband didn't answer, she asked, Why can't I hear her? And then, at last, she had understood.

It was just the two of them alone in the room now. Stacy's husband was at home with the boys. Stacy put her hand on the baby's cheeks, on her tiny hands. The skin was still warm. Her heart was still beating. The world was still turning on its axis.

Stacy's father blamed her mother for the accident, and he took her back to court to fight for full custody. He lost. Stacy and her brother visited him every other weekend. Their parents fought bitterly over school clothes and grades, their mother's bad neighborhood and their father's bad habits, and how they all talked and what they wore and who they slept with and everything they watched or listened to or ate or breathed (at her house, junk; at his house, poison).

They fought and fought.

But then their father got remarried and had two new kids and turned his attention toward them. Or so it had seemed at the time. Stacy was older now, and she understood that things were not always as they appeared.

The baby stirred. She turned and squinted up at Stacy before closing her eyes again. Stacy had always wanted a daughter. She pulled the baby out of the bassinet and into her arms.

Her father and stepmother still lived in her old hometown. Late one night, when she'd gone back for a visit, her father had had too much to drink and told her that the children had been millstones around his neck. She didn't know whether he meant Stacy and her brother, or their step-siblings, or all four of them combined, but her grandmother had told her not to ask a question if she didn't want to hear the answer.

Her mother retired and moved to Vermont with a man she met in an Introduction to Film class at the community college. It sounded like she spent most of her time walking their dogs and painting small, pristine snowscapes that she framed and hung around the house. Maybe she was happy, but it seemed like it had to be an act.

Sometimes Stacy would receive a package filled with carved wooden toys for the children and a long, handwritten letter, and she always turned the letters this way and that, looking for HELP ME spelled out in an acrostic or some other code, but she was never able to find the hidden message.

It was dark in the room. Stacy held the baby close. Later, her husband would bring the boys back to the hospital to visit.

She was awake, but her head was so heavy that she almost felt as if she were dreaming. She could still see the image of the woman in the white dress floating toward her. The woman had seemed like an angel, but she was just an ordinary mother, someone Stacy had seen months later carrying a plate of chocolate-frosted cupcakes toward the iron gates on the afternoon of the school bake sale.

As she crossed the yard, Stacy had watched her, feeling the metal of the house key, warm against her skin.

Acknowledgments

Grateful acknowledgment is made to the editors of the following publications in which these stories first appeared, sometimes in slightly different form:

Belle Ombre: "If the Orchid in Question Were a Pink and White Lady's Slipper"
The Big Windows Review: "Brute," "Three Sheets"
Birdland Journal: "A Hot Girl with a Bad Attitude," "Quarantine of the Hothouse Roses"
Blue Fifth Review: "Going in to Put Away His Laundry"
Boston Literary Magazine: "Porsche"
Chagrin River Review: "Jeopardy"
Contrary Magazine: "Caught"
Dime Show Review: "The Play"
Fiction365: "All These Questions"
Flock: "Scents/Sense/Cents"
The Forge Literary Magazine: "Wax"
Four Way Review: "White Flag"
Friday Flash Fiction: "One-Night Stand"
Halfway Down the Stairs: "The Costume Wedding," "Punch"
Harpur Palate: "Hope for the Future," "The Virtuoso (Circa 2018)"
Hive Avenue Literary Journal: "The Lawnmower"
The Ilanot Review: "Good Girls"
Litro Online: "Florida, 1993"

The Loch Raven Review: "The Body in the Bedroom"
Mojave River Review: "Fever Dreams"
Necessary Fiction: "Ventilation"
October Hill Magazine: "Around Her Neck"
Parhelion Literary Magazine: "Severance"
Per Contra: "Don't Panic"
The Petigru Review: "The Surrogate Wife"
Ponder Review: "Miscalculations"
Queen's Feminist Review: "The Wrist Corsage"
River and South Review: "Years Later (Revision)"
Santa Ana River Review: "Double You"
Sliver of Stone Magazine: "Empty Nests"
South 85 Journal: "Chappaquiddick"
Sou'wester: "90 Degrees, No A.C."
Star 82 Review: "False Alarm/Stop/Superior Court"
Superstition Review: "Small Kindness"
Terrain.org: "Dark Horse"
Thin Air Online: "My One and Only"
The Threepenny Review: "In the Air"
Two Hawks Quarterly: "The Rain in Brussels"
Uproot: "Savior"
Valparaiso Fiction Review: "Skin"
Watershed Review: "On Holiday"
The Westchester Review: "Souvenirs from Another Life"
Wilderness House Literary Review: "Four-in-Hand,"
"Fugitive," "Nobody Wants Your Heirlooms"
Wild Roof Journal: "Year of the Rat"
300 Days of Sun: "The Bigger Man"

Leah Browning is the author of *Two Good Ears* and *Loud Snow*, mini-books of flash fiction published by Silent Station Press, and *When the Sun Comes Out After Three Days of Rain*, a collection of poetry published by Kelsay Books. She is also the author of three short nonfiction books and six chapbooks of poetry and fiction. Browning's work has appeared in *Four Way Review*, *Harpur Palate*, *Valparaiso Fiction Review*, *The Threepenny Review*, *Necessary Fiction*, *Waxwing*, *Contrary Magazine*, *Passages North*, *Watershed Review*, *Newfound*, *The Forge Literary Magazine*, *Parhelion Literary Magazine*, *Flock*, *Superstition Review*, *Santa Ana River Review*, *Ponder Review*, *Thin Air Magazine*, *The Petigru Review*, *Belletrist Magazine*, *The Westchester Review*, *The Stillwater Review*, *The Broadkill Review*, and other literary journals and anthologies. In addition to writing, Browning has served as editor of the *Apple Valley Review* since 2005. She is originally from New Mexico.